CHRISTMAS IN MY HEART®

VIII

While Shepherds Watch'd

While shepherds watch'd their flocks by night,
All seated on the ground,
The angel of the Lord came down,
And glory shone around.

"Fear not!" said he, for mighty dread
Had seized their troubled mind,
"Glad tidings of great joy I bring
To you, and all mankind.

"To you, in David's town, this day
Is born of David's line,
The Saviour, who is Christ the Lord;
And this shall be the sign:

The heavenly Babe you there shall find
To human view display'd,
All meanly wrapt in swathing bands,
And in a manger laid."

Thus spake the seraph; and forthwith
Appeared a shining throng
Of angels, praising God, and thus
Address'd their joyful song:

"All glory be to God on high,
And to the earth be peace;
Good-will henceforth from heaven to men
Begin and never cease."

—*Nahum Tate*
(1652–1715)

FOCUS ON THE FAMILY®
presents

Christmas
IN MY
Heart

VIII

A TREASURY OF TIMELESS
CHRISTMAS STORIES

compiled and edited by
JOE L. WHEELER

TYNDALE HOUSE PUBLISHERS, INC. WHEATON, ILLINOIS

Published in association with the literary agency of Alive Communications, Inc., 1465 Kelly Johnson Blvd., Suite 320, Colorado Springs, CO 80920.

Library of Congress Cataloging-in-Publication Data

Printed in the United States of America

05   04   03   02   01   00   99

7   6   5   4   3   2   1

So dependent am I on his wisdom,
innovative ideas, helpfulness, and just *being
there* for me for all my questions, that it
would be easy to take him for granted.

But more than all the above, he is humble,
teachable, loyal, has a wonderful sense of
humor, and is a deeply committed Christian.

Thus, it gives me great pleasure to
dedicate *Christmas in My Heart 8* to my
dear friend Richard Coffen.

CONTENTS

ACKNOWLEDGMENTS

"Introduction: Tell Me a Story of Christmas," by Joseph Leininger Wheeler. Copyright © 1999. Printed by permission of the author.

"A Pint of Judgment," by Elizabeth Morrow. If anyone can provide knowledge of origin and first publication source of this old story or surviving heir, please relay this information to Joe Wheeler, in care of Tyndale House Publishers, P.O. Box 80, Wheaton, IL 60189.

"The Good Things of Life," by Arthur Gordon. Included in Gordon's anthology, *Through Many Windows*, 1983. Old Tappan, New Jersey: Fleming H. Revell Company. Reprinted by permission of the author.

"Christmas in the Heart," by Rachel Field. If anyone can provide knowledge of the origin and first publication source of this old story or surviving heir, please relay this information to Joe Wheeler, in care of Tyndale House Publishers, P.O. Box 80, Wheaton, IL 60189.

"Why the Chimes Rang," by Raymond Macdonald Alden. Included in Alden's anthology, *Why the Chimes Rang*, 1906, 1908, 1924. Indianapolis, Indiana: The Bobbs-Merrill Company.

"Merry Christmas, Mrs. Marigold," by Edward H. Imme. Copyright © 1964 by Concordia Publishing House. Used with permission.

"Feels Good in My Heart," by Wendy Miller. Copyright © 1999. Printed by permission of the author.

"A Girl like Me," by Nancy N. Rue. Published in *Brio*, December 1990. Reprinted by permission of the author.

"The Beloved House," by Annie Hamilton Donnell. Published in *Girls Own Annual*, 1914. London: William Clowes and Sons, Ltd.

"Special Delivery!" by Margaret E. Sangster Jr. If anyone can provide knowledge of origin and first publication source of this old story, please relay this information to Joe Wheeler, in care of Tyndale House Publishers, P.O. Box 80, Wheaton, IL 60189.

"Homemade Miracle," author unknown. If anyone can provide knowledge of authorship, origin, and first publication source of this old story, please relay this information to Joe Wheeler, in care of Tyndale House Publishers, P.O. Box 80, Wheaton, IL 60189.

"A Christmas Story," by Von M. Inger (translated by Hildegard Chan Epp). Translation used by permission.

"The Lord Gave the Word," from "The Tide of Fortune" by Stefan Zweig, "Georg Friedrich Haendel's Auferstehung" aus "Sternstunden der Menschheit" by Stefan Zweig. Reprinted by permission of William Verlag, AG, London, Zurich/Switzerland.

"Hermeda Sings a Carol," author unknown. If anyone can provide knowledge of authorship, origin, and first publication source of this old story, please relay this information to Joe Wheeler, in care of Tyndale House Publishers, P.O. Box 80, Wheaton, IL 60189.

"There's Magic in Believing," by Marguerite Brunner. Published in *Listen*, December 1970. Used by permission of Review and Herald Publishing Association, Inc., Hagerstown, Maryland 21740. If anyone knows of the whereabouts of the author or the author's heirs, please relay this information to Joe Wheeler, in care of Tyndale House Publishers, P.O. Box 80, Wheaton, IL 60189.

"The Christmas Room," by Gillette Jones. Published in *Christian Herald,* n.d. Reprinted by permission of Christian Herald Association.

"Legacy," by Joseph Leininger Wheeler. Copyright © 1999. Printed by permission of the author.

Joseph Leininger Wheeler

INTRODUCTION:
TELL ME A STORY
OF CHRISTMAS

Stories. *We never outgrow our love—our need—for them. Our earliest seasonal memories are not tied to "Tell me a sermon of Christmas" or "Tell me an essay of Christmas," but rather "Tell me a story of Christmas." I am convinced that a major reason for the success of the* Christmas in My Heart *series is the power of stories to convey values.* Christmas in My Heart *stories are about love, about hope, about redemption, about the difference that has been made in the world because of the Christ child. Many a sermon could be preached on these* subjects, and many have, but stories have an unusual power to touch the heart in a way few sermons can. Charles Colson explained the reason in a recent article in *Christianity Today:* "Stories change us because they reach the whole person, not just the cognitive faculty," he said. "As we read, we identify with characters who demonstrate courage and self-sacrifice, vicariously making choices along with them—and in the process, our own character is shaped" ("Moral Education After Monica," *Christianity Today,* March 1999).

Christ recognized full well the human yearning for stories. In fact, he rarely spoke without telling parables. I suspect that's because he knew that his hearers would quickly forget abstractions or homilies, but they'd *never* forget his stories.

Stories have power, but not just any story will do. Nor can story writing be taught effectively, for all the instruction and all the formulas in the world won't work unless the story itself does. Not even professional writers can explain why one story jells and another does not. There is a magical ingredient in compelling stories that no mortal yet has been able to define or isolate. That is why I maintain that there is no such thing as a great writer, only great stories. When I think about great stories, I am reminded of many of the selections included in the *Christmas in My Heart* series over the years. Some of them have had a seismic effect on those who read them—and some have found their way into the collections through what seemed to me to be divine intervention. Consider "The Tiny Foot," for example, a story that I found in stages. I wasn't able to complete it until I stumbled on an old paperback amidst thousands of other titles in a used bookstore. Somehow, in this vast blur, the good Lord drew me to the right shelf—and there, in very small print, were the words *Consultation Room* by Frederic Loomis. From that book, and from earlier transcripts of the story I had acquired through the years, came the complete story first published in *Christmas in*

My Heart, book 2. I was totally unprepared for the public's reaction to "The Tiny Foot." Requests to reprint it came in waves that have never ceased. Dr. James Dobson fell in love with it, twice using it as the Focus on the Family Christmas story of the year. A few years ago, at an East Coast book signing, a woman came up to my table to chat. After a while, she opened her purse and pulled out a battered copy of the first "The Tiny Foot" Christmas mailing from Focus on the Family. "I never let this leave my purse," she admitted to me. "It is one of the most precious things I own."

Another great story, "Charlie's Blanket," published in *Christmas in My Heart,* book 4, has also swept into the hearts of millions. Also sent out by Dr. Dobson at Christmas, this story's ministry is so vast it can't be quantified. "Charlie's Blanket" was sent to me, handwritten, by the previously unpublished author Wendy Miller. This Canadian mother of four, who had never before shared a story with anyone but her immediate family, sent me her story on a bet. A close relative had claimed she couldn't write well; she claimed she could. They agreed that I, unknowingly, was to decide the question. If I rejected "Charlie's Blanket," the relative would have won the bet. Instead, both my wife and I read the story and wept, agreeing that it *must* be included in the next Christmas anthology. God must have smiled at how a silly wager delivered a wonderful story to my doorstep. And now it has changed the lives of untold thousands who have been deeply moved by its message.

Then there is Cathy Miller's "Delayed Delivery," a story sent me by one of our Canadian readers after it had been awarded the top prize in a local newspaper contest. Had she not sent it to me, I would quite likely never have heard of it, but again the Lord was at work. After being published in *Christmas in My Heart,* book 2, Dr. Dobson used it as his Christmas story and thus it too has gone all around the world.

If you were to ask me how I choose the stories in a given anthology, as many interviewers have, I'd first get that sheepish look on my face, then admit that I have no surefire formula. The truth is that I am a rank sentimentalist who cries easily (an affliction I share with Dr. Dobson). If a story leaves me cold when I first read it, I am unlikely to ever touch it again, no matter how famous the author. On the other hand, if I find my eyes misting over and my hand reaching for a tissue, then that story—no matter *who* wrote it—is destined for an anthology down the line.

In addition to choosing stories that have moved me, I also choose stories that have deeply moved others. When readers all across the continent write me, telling me how a given story means so much to them and their families and urging me to include it in an upcoming collection, I pay attention. The more people who write me about a story, the more likely I am to consider including it in an anthology.

THE CHRIST FACTOR

Most Santa Claus stories leave me cold—not because I don't like Santa Claus but because Santa stories tend to lack the transformational element that can only come from God. As most readers of this series know, the stories in all the *Christmas in My Heart* collections are Christ-centered rather than Santa-centered. This doesn't mean that I have anything against Santa Claus *per se*. In fact, my preacher father dressed up in his Santa Claus suit every Christmas for us kids. But we were never permitted to forget for a moment that Christmas without Christ was a travesty. Thus, many of our most loved Christmas stories, such as this collection's "There Is Magic in Believing," include Santa Claus in a supporting role, but rarely, if ever, as the lead.

When God enters a story, even if he is only implied through

Christian-based values, there is an opportunity for miracles to take place, for the heart to be softened and reborn.

Christ-centered stories don't need to be overtly preachy—I maintain that the best ones let their story lines carry their own freight. An example: "Tell Me a Story of Christmas," written by the late Bill Vaughan and featured in *Christmas in My Heart,* book 2. In this tale, a little girl is sitting on her father's lap, asking him to tell her a story of Christmas. Wanting above all else to make her happy, he starts a story about elves at the North Pole. She interrupts him, whispering, "I'm tired of elves."

The father tries again, this time with a story about a Christmas puppy, much like her own Pinky. She sighs, "I'm tired of puppies. I love Pinky, of course. I mean story puppies."

The father pauses, then launches into a story of a plain little Christmas tree that no one wants. Disappointed, the little girl breaks in. "No trees, Daddy. . . . We have a tree at school and at Sunday school and at the supermarket and downstairs and a little one in my room. I am very tired of trees."

He then starts to tell her the story of Rudolph, but his daughter just looks at him reproachfully. Seeing she is tired of reindeer stories, too, he asks if she'd like to hear a true Christmas story, one from his own childhood. "Yes, Daddy," she says quietly. "But not right now. Not tonight."

His repertoire exhausted, the father hopes his little girl will fall asleep so he will be let off the hook. But no, once more she murmurs, "Tell me a story of Christmas."

Vaughan concludes with these moving words: "Then it was as though he could read the words, so firmly were they in his memory. Still holding her hand, he leans back:

'And it came to pass in those days, that there went out a decree from Caesar Augustus, that all the world should be taxed. . . .'

Her hand tightened a bit in his, and he told her a story of Christmas."

I often read that story for groups and radio audiences because its message is so powerful: just as the little girl is not satisfied with any of the Christmas stories until her father tells the ultimate one about the birth of Christ, so we find little meaning in Christmas stories that fail to incorporate the real reason we celebrate Christmas—the birth of Christ.

ABOUT THE EIGHTH COLLECTION

The stories in this eighth collection are among the most moving I have ever read. We have brought back Arthur Gordon (you will remember his "Miraculous Staircase" and "First Crèche" in *Christmas in My Heart,* books 6 and 7); Wendy Miller (who could possibly forget her now famous and gathered-to-the-heart "Charlie's Blanket" in *Christmas in My Heart,* book 4?); Nancy Rue (many fell in love with her "Red Envelope" in *Christmas in My Heart,* book 7); Annie Hamilton Donnell (who is by now a dear friend thanks to her "Running Away from Christmas" and "Rebecca's Only Way" in *Christmas in My Heart,* books 2 and 3); and Margaret Sangster Jr. (cherished indeed for "The Littlest Orphan," "Lonely Tree," "With a Star on Top," and "Small Things" in *Christmas in My Heart,* books 1, 3, 5, and 6). "New" authors we are introducing this year include Elizabeth Morrow, Rachel Field, Raymond Macdonald Alden, Edward H. Imme, Von M. Inger, Stefan Zweig, Marguerite Brunner, and Gillette Jones.

The write-in story of the year? Unquestionably, Rachel Field's classic, "Christmas in the Heart"!

CODA

When the first *Christmas in My Heart* collection was published seven Christmases ago, there was no number on the book. There was a good reason for that: it was intended as a onetime book project. Once done with it, I planned to go back to the college classroom and move on to other projects. But God had other plans. When the book ran through two printings, the editor asked me if I could manage to put another collection together. I said I thought I could. Thus followed *Christmas in My Heart,* books 2–7.

The initial collections seemed to fill a niche. Letters poured in from readers urging me to keep the anthologies coming. I worried about running out of good stories. But God had an answer: from that day to this, so many of you have crammed my mailbox with your favorite stories that I now have more great Christmas stories to choose from than I did at the beginning.

This eighth Christmas collection carries, for the first time, the Focus on the Family/Tyndale House dual imprint. You have helped to make this possible by the great appreciation you have expressed in hundreds and hundreds of letters sent via Focus on the Family urging me to continue this annual tradition. As long as people like you continue to buy these collections for yourselves and those on your stocking lists every Christmas, and as long as the good Lord blesses our work and grants us health and strength, then these annual collections are likely to continue.

Ilook forward to hearing from you! Please do keep the stories, responses, and suggestions coming. And not just for Christmas stories—I am putting together collections centered around other themes as well. You may reach me by writing:

Joe L. Wheeler, Ph.D.
c/o Tyndale House Publishers
351 Executive Drive
Wheaton, IL 60189-0080

Elizabeth Morrow

A PINT OF
JUDGMENT

Seven-year-old Sally wanted to give her mother an extra-special Christmas this year. At the end of Mother's Christmas list, handwritten, were the words: "A quart of judgment"—but Mother had admitted she'd be satisfied with just a pint.

So Sally set out to get it for her.

Early in this century, this story became one of the most beloved Christmas stories in America, then gradually receded out of public notice. I think you'll agree it deserves to come back.

The Tucker family made out lists of what they wanted for Christmas. They did not trust to Santa Claus's taste or the wisdom of aunts and uncles in such an important matter. By the first week in December everybody had written out what he or she hoped to receive.

Sally, who was seven, when she could only print had sent little slips of paper up the chimney with her desires plainly set forth. She had wondered sometimes if neatly written requests like Ellen's were not more effective than the printed ones. Ellen was eight. She had asked last year for a muff, and Santa had sent it.

Mother always explained that one should not expect to get all the things on the list; "only what you want most, dear, and sometimes you have to wait till you are older for those."

For several years Sally had asked for a lamb, and she had almost given up hope of finding one tied to her stocking on Christmas morning. She had also asked for a white cat and a dove, and they had not come either. Instead a bowl of goldfish had been received. Now she wrote so plainly that there was no excuse for misunderstandings like this.

Derek still printed his list—he was only six, and yet he had received an Indian suit the very first time he asked for it. It was puzzling.

Caroline, called "Lovey" for short, just stood on the hearth rug and shouted, "Dolly! Bow wow!" but anybody with Santa Claus's experience would know that rag dolls and woolly dogs were the proper presents for a four-year-old.

The lists were useful too in helping one to decide what to make for Father and Mother and the others for Christmas. The little Tuckers had been brought up by their grandmother in the belief that a present you made yourself was far superior to one bought in a store. Mother always asked for a great many things the children could make. She was always wanting knitted washcloths, pincushion covers, blotters, and penwipers. Father needed pipe cleaners, calendars, and decorated match boxes.

This year Sally longed to do something quite different for her mother. She was very envious of Ellen, who had started a small towel as her present and was pulling threads for a fringed end.

"Oh! Ellen! How lovely that is!" she sighed. "It is a real grown-up present, just as if Aunt Elsie had made it."

"And it isn't half done yet," Ellen answered proudly. "Grandma is helping me with cross-stitch letters in blue and red for one end."

"If I could only make something nice like that! Can't you think of something for me?"

"A hemmed handkerchief?" suggested Ellen.

"Oh no! Mother has lots of handkerchiefs."

"Yes, but when I gave her one for her birthday, she said she had never had enough handkerchiefs. They were like asparagus."

"They don't look like asparagus," Sally replied, loath to criticize her mother but evidently confused. "Anyway, I don't want to give her a handkerchief."

"A penwiper?"

"No, I'm giving Father that."

"A new pincushion cover?"

"Oh no, Ellen! I'm sick of those presents. I want it to be a big, lovely—something—a great surprise."

Ellen thought a minute. She was usually resourceful, and she did not like to fail her little sister. They had both been earning money all through November, and perhaps this was a time to *buy* a present for Mother—even if Grandma disapproved.

"I know that Mother has made out a new list," she said. "She and Father were laughing about it last night in the library. Let's go and see if it is there."

They found two pieces of paper on the desk, unmistakably

lists. They were typewritten. Father's was very short: "Anything wrapped up in tissue paper with a red ribbon around it."

"Isn't Father funny?" giggled Ellen. "I'd like to fool him and do up a dead mouse for his stocking."

Mother had filled a full page with her wants. Ellen read out slowly:

Pair of Old English silver peppers
Fur coat—"Father will give her that."
Umbrella
Robert Frost's poems
Silk stockings
Muffin tins
Small watering pot for houseplants
Handkerchiefs
Guest towels

"Aren't you glad she asked for that?" Sally broke in.

Knitted washcloths
A red pencil
A blue pencil
Ink eraser
Pen holders
Rubber bands
Hot water bag cover
A quart of judgment

This last item was scribbled in pencil at the bottom of the sheet.

As Ellen finished reading, she said with what Sally called her "Little-mother air," "You needn't worry at all about Mother's present. There are lots of things here you could make for her.

Couldn't you do a hot water bag cover if Grandma cut it out for you? I'm sure you could. You take a nice soft piece of old flannel . . ."

"No! No! Nothing made out of old flannel!" cried Sally. "That's such a baby thing. I want it to be different—and a great surprise. I wish I could give her the silver peppers. . . . That's the first thing on her list; but I've only got two dollars and three cents in my bank, and I'm afraid that's not enough."

"Oh! It isn't the peppers she wants most!" cried Ellen. "It's the *last* thing she wrote down—that 'quart of judgment.' I know for I heard her tell Father, 'I need that more than anything else . . . even a pint would help.' And then they both laughed."

"What is judgment?" asked Sally.

"It's what the judge gives—a judgment," her sister answered. "It must be something to do with the law."

"Then I know it would cost more than two dollars and three cents," said Sally. "Father said the other day that nothing was so expensive as the law."

"But she only asked for a pint," Ellen objected. "A pint of anything couldn't be very expensive, unless it was rubies and diamonds."

"She wanted a *quart,*" Sally corrected. "And she just said that afterward about a pint helping because she knew a whole quart would be too much for us to buy."

"A hot water bag cover would be lots easier," cautioned Ellen.

"I don't want it to be easy!" cried Sally. "I want it to be what she wants!"

"Well, perhaps you could get it cheap from Uncle John," Ellen suggested. "He's a lawyer—and he's coming to dinner tonight, so you could ask him."

Sally was not afraid to ask Uncle John anything. He never laughed at her or teased her as Uncle Tom sometimes did, and he always talked to her as if she were grown up. On any vexed question he always sided with her and Ellen. He had even been known to say before Mother that coconut cake was good for children and that seven-thirty for big girls of seven and eight was a disgracefully early bedtime. He thought arctics unnecessary in winter, and when a picnic was planned, he always knew it would be a fine day.

Sally drew him into the little library that evening and shut the door carefully.

"Is it something very important?" he asked as they seated themselves on the sofa.

"Yes," she answered. "Awfully important. It's a secret. You won't tell, will you?"

"No, cross my heart and swear. What is it?"

"It's–it's . . . Oh, Uncle John—what is judgment? I must get some."

"Judgment? That *is* an important question, my dear." Uncle John seemed puzzled for a moment. "And it is hard to answer. Why do you bother about that now? You have your whole life to get it. . . . Come to me again when you're eighteen."

"But I can't wait so long. I must get it right away. Mother wants it for a Christmas present. She put on her list, 'A quart of judgment.' She said even a pint would help."

Uncle John laughed. He threw back his head and shouted. Sally had never seen him laugh so hard. He shook the sofa with his mirth, and tears rolled down his cheeks. He didn't stop until he saw that Sally was hurt—and even then a whirlwind of chuckles seized him occasionally.

"I'm not laughing at you, Sally darling," he explained at last, patting her shoulder affectionately, "but at your mother. She doesn't need judgment. She has it. She always has had it. She's a mighty fine woman—your mother. She must have put that on her list as a joke."

"Oh no! Excuse me, Uncle John," Sally protested. "She told

14

Father she wanted it more than anything else. Wouldn't it be a good Christmas present?"

"Perfectly swell," her uncle answered. "The most useful. If you have any left over, give me some."

"Why, I was going to ask you to sell me some," Sally explained. "Ellen said you would surely have it."

Just then Mother called, "Ellen! Sally! Bedtime. Hurry, dears. It's twenty minutes to eight already."

"Bother!" exclaimed Sally. "I'm always having to go to bed. But please tell me where I can get it. At Macy's? Delia is taking us to town tomorrow."

"No, my dear," he answered. "Macy's sells almost everything, but not that. It doesn't come by the yard."

"Girls!" Mother's voice again.

"Oh! Quick, Uncle John," whispered Sally. "Mother's coming. I'll have to go. Just tell me. What *is* judgment?"

"It is *sense,* Sally," he answered, quite solemn and serious now. "Common sense. But it takes a lot . . ." He could not finish the sentence for at this point Mother opened the door and carried Sally off to bed.

The little girl snuggled down under the sheets very happily. Uncle John had cleared her mind of all doubt. She had only time for an ecstatic whisper to Ellen before Delia put out the light:

"It's all right about Mother's present. Uncle John said it would be 'swell.'" Then she began to calculate: "If it is just cents, common cents, I have ever so many in my bank, and I can earn some more. Perhaps I have enough already."

With this delicious hope she fell asleep.

The first thing after breakfast the next morning she opened her bank. It was in the shape of a fat man sitting in a chair. When you put a penny in his hand, he nodded his head in gratitude as

the money slipped into his safety box. Sally unscrewed the bottom of this, and two dollars and three cents rolled out. It was not
all in pennies. There were several nickels, three dimes, two quarters and a fifty-cent piece. It made a rich-looking pile. Sally ran
to the kitchen for a pint cup and then up to the nursery to pour
her wealth into it. No one was there in the room to hear her cry
of disappointment. The coins did not reach to the "half" mark on
the measure.

But there was still hope. The half dollar and quarters when
they were changed would lift the level, of course. She put all the
silver into her pocket and consulted Ellen.

Her sister had passed the penny-bank stage and kept her
money in a blue leather purse, which was a proud possession.
Aunt Elsie had given it to her last Christmas. It had two compart-
ments and a small looking glass—but there was very little money
in it now. Ellen had already bought a good many presents. She
was only able to change one quarter and one dime.

"Let's ask Derek," she said. "He loves to open his bank
because he can use the screwdriver of his tool set."

Derek was delighted to show his savings—forty-five
cents—but he was reluctant to give them all up for one quarter
and two dimes. It would mean only three pieces to drop into the
chimney of the little red house, which was his bank.

"They don't clink at all," he complained, experimenting with
the coins Sally held out. "You'll take all my money. I won't have
hardly anything."

"You'll have *just* as much money to spend," explained Ellen.

"Yes," Derek admitted, "but not to jingle. I like the jingle.
It sounds so much more."

He finally decided to change one nickel and one dime.

Then Grandma changed a dime, and Sally had sixty pennies all
together to put into the pint cup. They brought the pile up about
an inch.

When father came home that night she asked him to change the fifty-cent piece, the quarter, and the three nickels, but he did not have ninety cents in pennies and said that he could not get them until Monday, and now it was only Saturday.

"You understand, Sally," he explained looking down into his little daughter's anxious face, "you don't have any more money after this is changed. It only looks more."

"I know, but I want it that way," she answered.

On Monday night he brought her the change, and it made a full inch more of money in the cup. Still it was less than half a pint. Sally confided her discouragement to Ellen.

"Are you sure," asked her sister, "that it was this kind of present Mother wanted? She never asked for money before."

"I'm sure," Sally replied. "Uncle John said it was *cents* and that it would take a lot. Besides she prayed for it in church yesterday—so she must want it awfully."

"Prayed for it!" exclaimed Ellen in surprise.

"Yes. I heard her. It's that prayer we all say together. She asked God for 'two cents of all thy mercies.'"

"But if she wants a whole pint, why did she only ask for 'two cents'?" demanded the practical Ellen.

"I don't know," Sally answered. "Perhaps she thought it would be greedy. Mother is never greedy."

For several days things were at a standstill. Ellen caught a cold and passed it on to Sally and Derek. They were all put to bed and could do very little Christmas work. While Mother read aloud to them, Sally finished her penwiper for Father and decorated a blotter for Uncle John—but sewing on Grandma's pincushion cover was difficult because the pillow at Sally's back kept slipping, and she couldn't keep the needle straight. There seemed no way of adding anything to the pint cup.

"Mother, how could I earn some money quickly before Christmas?" Sally asked the first day that she was up.

"You have already earned a good deal, dear," Mother said. "Do you really need more?"

"Yes, Mother, lots more."

"How about getting 100 in your number work? Father gives you a dime every time you do that."

"Yes," sighed Sally, "but it's very hard to get all the examples right. Don't you think that when I get all right but one he might give me nine cents?"

"No," said Mother, laughing. "Your father believes that nothing is good in arithmetic but 100."

She did earn one dime that way and then school closed, leaving no hope for anything more before Christmas.

On the twentieth of December there was a windfall. Aunt Elsie, who usually spent the holidays with them, was in the South, and she sent Mother four dollars—one for each child for a Christmas present. "She told me to buy something for you," Mother explained, "but I thought perhaps you might like to spend the money yourselves—later on—during vacation."

"Oh! I'd like my dollar right away!" cried Sally delightedly. "And," she added rather shamefacedly, "Lovey is so little . . . do you think she needs all her money? Couldn't she give me half hers?"

"Why, Sally, I'm surprised at you!" her mother answered. "I can't take your little sister's share for you. It wouldn't be fair. I am buying a new *Benjamin Bunny* for Lovey."

Aunt Elsie's gift brought the pennies in the pint cup a little above the half mark.

On the twenty-first Sally earned five cents by sweeping off the back porch. This had been a regular source of revenue in the fall, but when the dead leaves gave place to snow, Mother forbade the sweeping. On the twenty-first there was no snow, and Sally was allowed to go out with her little broom.

On the twenty-second Ellen and Sally went to a birthday

party, and Sally found a shiny bright dime in her piece of birthday cake. This helped a little. She and Ellen spent all their spare moments in shaking up the pennies in the pint measure—but they could not bring the level much above "one half." Ellen was as excited over the plan now as Sally, and she generously added her last four cents to the pile.

On the twenty-third Sally made a final desperate effort. "Mother," she said, "Uncle John is coming to dinner again tonight. Do you think he would be willing to give me my birthday dollar now?"

Mother smiled as she answered slowly, "But your birthday isn't till June. Isn't it rather strange to ask for your present so long ahead? Where is all this money going to?"

"It's a secret! My special secret!" cried the little girl, taking her mother's reply for consent.

Uncle John gave her the dollar. She hugged and kissed him with delight, and he said, "Let me always be your banker, Sally. I'm sorry you are so hard up, but don't take any wooden nickels."

"Wooden nickels," she repeated slowly. "What are they? Perhaps they would fill up the bottom—"

"Of your purse?" Uncle John finished the sentence for her. "No, no, my dear. They are a very poor bottom for anything—and they are worse on top."

"It wasn't my purse," said Sally. "It was—but it's a secret."

When Father changed the birthday dollar into pennies he said, "You are getting to be a regular little miser, my dear. I don't understand it. Where is all this money going to?"

"That's just what Mother asked," Sally answered. "It's a secret. You'll know on Christmas. Oh, Father, I think I have enough now!"

"But she hadn't. The pennies seemed to melt away as they fell into the measure. She and Ellen took them all out three times and put them back again, shaking them sideways and forwards, but it was no use. They looked like a mountain on the nursery floor, but they shrank in size the moment they were put inside that big cup. The mark stood obstinately below "three quarters."

"Oh! Ellen!" sobbed Sally after the third attempt. "Not even a pint! It's a horrid mean little present! All my presents are horrid. I never can give nice things like you! Oh, dear, what shall I do?"

"Don't cry, Sally—please don't," said Ellen, trying to comfort her little sister. "It's not a horrid present. It will look lovely when you put tissue paper around it and lots of red ribbon and a card. It *sounds* so much more than it looks," Ellen went on, giving the cup a vigorous jerk. "Why don't you print on your card 'Shake well before opening,' like our cough mixture?"

"I might," assented Sally, only partly reassured.

She had believed up to the last moment that she would be able to carry out her plan. It was vaguely associated in her mind with a miracle. Anything might happen at Christmastime, but this year she had hoped for too much. It was so late now however that there was nothing to do but make the outside of her gift look as attractive as possible. She and Ellen spent most of the afternoon before Christmas wrapping up their presents. The pint cup was a little awkward in shape, but they had it well covered and the red satin ribbon gathered tight at the top before Grandma made the final bow. It was a real rosette, for Sally had asked for something special.

Christmas Eve was almost more fun than Christmas. The Tuckers made a ceremony of hanging up their stockings. The whole family formed a line in the upper hall with Father at the head, the youngest child on his back, and then they marched downstairs keeping step to a Christmas chant. It was a homemade nonsense verse with a chorus of "Doodley-doodley, doodley-doo!" which everybody shouted. By the time they reached the living room the line was in wild spirits.

The stockings were always hung in the same places. Father had the big armchair to the right of the fireplace and Mother the large mahogany chair opposite it. Lovey had a small white chair borrowed from the nursery. Derek tied his sock to the hook that usually held the fire tongs above the wood basket (it was a very inconvenient place but he liked it), and Ellen and Sally divided the sofa.

After the stockings were put up, one of the children recited the Bible verses, "And there were in the same country shepherds abiding in the field, keeping watch over their flock by night," through "Mary kept all these things, and pondered them in her heart." Sally had said the verses last Christmas—Ellen the year before—and now it was Derek's turn. He only forgot once and Ellen prompted him softly.

Then they all sang "Holy Night"—and Father read "'Twas the Night before Christmas." Last of all, the children distributed their gifts for the family—with a great many stern directions: "Mother, you won't look at this till tomorrow, will you?" "Father, you promise not to peek." Then they went up to bed, and by morning Father and Mother and Santa Claus had the stockings stuffed full of things.

It went off as usual this year, but through all the singing and shouting Sally had twinges of disappointment thinking of Mother's unfinished present. She had squeezed it into Mother's stocking with some difficulty. Then came Ellen's lovely towel and on top of that Derek's calendar, which he had made in school.

There was a family rule at the Tuckers' that stockings were not opened until after breakfast. Mother said that presents on an empty stomach were bad for temper and digestion, and though it was hard to swallow your cereal Christmas morning, the children knew it was no use protesting.

The first sight of the living room was wonderful. The place

had completely changed overnight. Of course the stockings were knobby with unknown delights, and there were packages everywhere, on the tables and chairs, and on the floor big express boxes that had come from distant places, marked "Do Not Open until Christmas."

Some presents are of such unmistakable shape that they cannot be hidden. Last year Derek had jumped right onto his rocking horse shouting, "It's mine! I know it's mine!" This morning he caught sight of a drum and looked no further. Lovey fell upon a white plush bunny. A lovely pink parasol was sticking out of the top of Sally's stocking and Ellen had a blue one. They just unfurled them over their heads and then watched Father and Mother unwrapping their presents.

The girls felt Derek and Lovey were very young because they emptied their stockings without a look toward the two big armchairs. That was the most thrilling moment, when your own offering came to view and Mother said, "Just what I wanted!" or Father, "How did you know I needed a penwiper?"

Mother always opened the children's presents first. She was untying the red ribbon on Ellen's towel now and reading the card that said: "Every stitch a stitch of love." As she pulled off the tissue paper she exclaimed, "What beautiful work! What exquisite little stitches! Ellen—I am proud of you. This is a charming guest towel. Thank you, dear, so much."

"Grandma marked the cross-stitch for me," explained Ellen, "but I did all the rest myself."

Sally shivered with excitement as Mother's hand went down into her stocking again and tugged at the tin cup.

"Here is something very heavy," she said. "I can't guess what it is, and the card says: 'Merry Christmas to Mother from Sally. Shake well before opening.' Is it medicine or cologne?"

Nobody remembered just what happened after that. Perhaps Grandma's bow was not tied tightly enough, perhaps Mother

tilted the cup as she shook it, but in a moment all the pennies
were on the floor. They rolled everywhere, past the chairs, into
the grate, under the sofa and onto the remotest corners of the
room. There was a terrific scramble. Father and Mother and Ellen
and Sally and Derek, even Grandma and Lovey got down on
their hands and knees to pick them up. They bumped elbows and
knocked heads together, and this onrush sent the coins flying
everywhere. The harder they were chased, the more perversely
they hid themselves. Out of the hubbub Mother cried, "Sally,
dear, what is this? I don't understand. All your Christmas money
for me? Darling, I can't take it."

Sally flung herself into her mother's arms with a sob. "Oh, you
must!" she begged. "I'm sorry it's not a whole pint. I tried so
hard. You said—you said you wanted it most of all."

"Most of all?"

"Yes, judgment, cents. Uncle John said it was cents. You said
even a pint would help. Won't half a pint be some good?"

Father and Mother and Grandma all laughed then. Father
laughed almost as hard as Uncle John did when he first heard of
Mother's list, and he declared that he was going to take Sally into
the bank as a partner. But Mother lifted the little girl into her lap
and whispered, "It's the most wonderful present I ever had.
There's nothing so wonderful as sense—except love."

Arthur Gordon

THE GOOD THINGS
OF LIFE

***

They *were coming back this Christmas morning—coming back to where it had all started. Since that time, growing fame had come to him, changed him, warped him. Self had pushed God aside.* Would the little church be on her side? *Mary wondered.*

Near the crest of the hill he felt the rear wheels of the car spin for half a second, and he felt a flash of the unreasonable irritability that had been plaguing him lately. He said, a bit grimly, "Good thing it didn't snow more than an inch or two. We'd be in trouble if it had."

His wife was driving. She often did, so that he could make notes for a sermon or catch up on his endless correspondence by dictating into the tape recorder he had had built into the car. Now she looked out at the woods and fields gleaming in the morning sunlight. "It's pretty, though. And Christmassy. We haven't had a white Christmas like this in years."

He gave her an amused and affectionate glance. "You always see the best side of things, don't you, my love?"

"Well, after hearing you urge umpteen congregations to do precisely that . . ."

Arnold Barclay smiled, and some of the lines of tension and fatigue went out of his face. "Remember the bargain we made twenty years ago? I'd do the preaching, and you'd do the practicing."

Her mouth curved faintly. "I remember."

They came to a crossroads, and he found that after all these years he still remembered the sign: Littlefield, 1 Mile. He said, "How's the time?"

She glanced at the diamond watch on her wrist—his present to her this year. "A little after ten."

He leaned forward and switched on the radio. In a moment his own voice, strong and resonant, filled the car, preaching a Christmas sermon prepared and recorded weeks before. He listened to a sentence or two, then smiled sheepishly and turned it off. "Just wanted to hear how I sounded."

"You sound fine," Mary Barclay said. "You always do."

They passed a farmhouse, the new snow sparkling like diamonds on the roof, the Christmas wreath gay against the front door. "Who lived there?" he asked. "Peterson, wasn't it? No, Johannsen."

"That's right," his wife said. "Eric Johannsen. Remember the night he made you hold the lantern while the calf was born?"

"Do I ever!" He rubbed his forehead wearily. "About this new television proposition, Mary. What do you think? It would be an extra load, I know. But I'd be reaching an enormous audience. The biggest—"

She put her hand on his arm. "Darling, it's Christmas Day. Can't we talk about it later?"

"Why, sure," he said, but something in him was offended all the same. The television proposal was important. Why, in fifteen minutes he would reach ten times as many people as Saint Paul had reached in a lifetime! He said, "How many people did the Littlefield church hold, Mary? About a hundred, wasn't it?"

"Ninety-six," his wife said. "To be exact."

"Ninety-six!" He gave a rueful laugh. "Quite a change of pace."

It was that, all right. It was years since he had preached in anything but metropolitan churches. The Littlefield parish had been the beginning. Now, on Christmas morning, he was going back. Back for an hour or two, to stand in the little pulpit where he had preached his first hesitant, fumbling sermon twenty years ago.

He let his head fall back against the seat and closed his eyes. The decision to go back had not been his, really; it had been Mary's. She handled all his appointments, screening the innumerable invitations to preach or speak. A month ago she had come to him. There was a request, she said, for him to go back to Littlefield and preach a sermon on Christmas morning.

"Littlefield?" he had said, incredulous. "What about that Washington invitation?" He had been asked to preach to a congregation that would, he knew, include senators and cabinet members.

"We haven't answered it yet," she said. "We could drive to Littlefield on Christmas morning if we got up early enough. . . ."

He had stared at her. "You mean, you think we *ought* to go back there?"

She had looked back at him calmly. "That's up to you, Arnold." But he knew what she wanted him to say.

Making such a decision wasn't so hard at the moment, he thought wearily. Not resenting afterward—that was the difficult part. Maybe it wouldn't be so bad. The church would be horribly overcrowded, the congregation would be mostly farmers, but . . .

The car stopped; he opened his eyes.

They were at the church, all right. There it sat by the side of the road, just as it always had—if anything, it looked smaller than he remembered it. Around it the fields stretched away, white and unbroken, to the neighboring farmhouses. But there were no cars, there was no crowd, there was no sign of anyone. The church was shuttered and silent.

He looked at Mary, bewildered. She did not seem surprised. She pushed open the car door. "Let's go inside, shall we? I still have a key."

The church was cold. Standing in the icy gloom, he could see his breath steam in the gray light. He said, and his voice sounded strange, "Where is everybody? You said there was a request . . ."

"There was a request," Mary said. "From me." She moved forward slowly until she was standing by the pulpit. "Arnold," she said, "the finest sermon I ever heard you preach was right here in this church. It was your first Christmas sermon; we hadn't been married long. You didn't know our first baby was on the way—but I did. Maybe that's why I remember so well what you said.

"You said that God had tried every way possible to get through to people. He tried prophets and miracles and revelations—and nothing worked. So then He said, '"I'll send them something they can't fail to understand. I'll send them the simplest and yet the most wonderful thing in all My creation. I'll send them a Baby. . . .' Do you remember that?"

He nodded wordlessly.

"Well," she said, "I heard that they had no minister here now, so I knew they wouldn't be having a service this morning. And I thought . . . well, I thought it might be good for . . . for both of us if you could preach that sermon again. Right here, where your ministry began. I just thought . . ."

Her voice trailed off, but he knew what she meant. He knew what she was trying to tell him, although she was too loyal and too kind to say it in words. That he had gotten away from the sources of his strength. That as success had come to him, as his reputation had grown larger, some things in him had grown smaller. The selflessness. The humility. The most important things of all.

He stood there, silent, seeing himself with a terrifying clarity: the pride, the ambition, the hunger for larger and larger audiences. Not for the glory of God. For the glory of Arnold Barclay.

He clenched his fists, feeling panic grip him, a sense of terror and guilt unlike anything he had ever known. Then faintly, underneath the panic, something else stirred. He glanced around the little church. She was right, Mary was right, and perhaps it wasn't too late. Perhaps here, now, he could rededicate himself. . . .

Abruptly he stripped off his overcoat, tossed it across the back of a pew. He reached out and took both of Mary's hands. He heard himself laugh, an eager, boyish laugh. "We'll do it! We'll do it just the way we used to! You open the shutters; that was your job, remember? I'll start the furnace. We'll have a Christmas service just for the two of us. I'll preach that sermon, all for you!"

She turned quickly to the nearest window, raised it, began fumbling with the catch that held the shutters. He opened the door that led to the cellar steps. Down in the frigid basement he found the furnace squatting, as black and malevolent as ever. He flung open the iron door. No fire was laid, but along the wall wood was stacked, and kindling, and newspapers.

He began to crumple papers and thrust them into the furnace, heedless of the soot that blackened his fingers. Overhead he heard the sound that made him pause. Mary was trying the wheezy old melodeon. "Ring the bell, too," he shouted up the stairs. "We might as well do the job right!"

He heard her laugh. A moment later, high in the belfry, the bell began to ring. Its tone was as clear and resonant as ever, and the sound brought back a flood of memories: the baptisms, the burials, the Sunday dinners at the old farmhouses, the honesty and brusqueness and simple goodness of the people.

He stood there, listening, until the bell was silent. Then he struck a match and held it to the newspapers. Smoke curled reluctantly. He reached up, adjusted the old damper, tried again. This time a tongue of flame flickered. For perhaps five minutes he watched it, hovering over it, blowing on it. When he was sure that it was kindled, he went back up the cellar steps.

The church was a blaze of sunlight. Where the window glass was clear, millions of dust motes whirled and danced; where there were panes of stained glass, the rays fell on the old floor in pools of ruby and topaz and amethyst. Mary was standing at the church door. "Arnold," she said, "come here."

He went and stood beside her. After the darkness of the cellar, the sun on the snow was so bright that he couldn't see anything.

"Look," she said in a whisper. "They're coming."

Cupping his hands round his eyes, he stared out across the glistening whiteness, and he saw that she was right. They were coming. Across the fields. Down the roads. Some on foot. Some in cars. They were coming, he knew, not to hear him, not to hear any preacher, however great. They were coming because it was Christmas Day, and this was their church, and its bell was calling them. They were coming because they wanted someone to give them the ancient message, to tell them the good news.

He stood there with his arm round his wife's shoulders and the soot black on his face and the overflowing happiness in his heart. "Merry Christmas," he said. "Merry Christmas. And thank you. Thank you, darling."

Arthur Gordon
1912

During his long and illustrious career, Gordon has edited such renowned journals as *Good Housekeeping, Cosmopolitan,* and *Guideposts.* Along the way, besides penning over two hundred of some of the finest short stories of our time, he also somehow found time to write books, such as *Reprisal, Norman Vincent Peale: Minister to Millions, Red Carpet at the White House, A Touch of Wonder,* and *Through Many Windows.* Today, he and his wife, Pamela, still live on the Georgia coast he has loved since he was a child. Readers will remember his unforgettable stories, "The Miraculous Staircase" in *Christmas in My Heart,* book 6, and "The First Crèche" in *Christmas in My Heart,* book 7. What a joy to include another story of his in this collection!

Rachel Field

CHRISTMAS IN
THE HEART

---

*Two little girls, trudging up a hill to the Lutheran Home
for the Aged that late December evening, took seriously
their mission: to deliver safely that precious Christmas
basket. Little did they know that an even greater present
awaited* them—*a story to sing down through the years.
So many have written in, urging me to include this
deeply moving story in our series, that we decided to
include it in this year's collection.*

Years ago and years ago two little girls trudged up a long hill in the twilight of late December. They carried a basket between them, and one was I, and one was Helga Swanson. The smell of warm coffee cake and braided cinnamon bread and little brown twists like deer horns comes back to me now from that remembered basket. Sweeter than all the perfumes of Arabia that fragrance reached our half-frozen noses, yet we never lifted the folded napkin, for we took our responsibility seriously. Helga's mother and grandmother had spent the better part of three days over that Christmas baking, and we had been chosen to deliver it and help trim the tree at the Lutheran Home on the hill above Fallen Leaf Lake.

"We must hurry," Helga said. "They've lighted the parlors already."

Four squares of brightness drew us like magnets up that steep hill. Our feet went crunching through the icy road ruts as we kept step together except when we stopped to change hands with the basket.

I could hardly see Helga's face for the darkness, but I felt her warm, vigorous presence beside me in her tightly buttoned coat and knitted tam that half covered her fair braids. I would be seven in another month, and she had been eight last March when we had moved from the state of Maine to Minnesota. It had seemed strange and a little frightening to me then to hear so many people speaking to one another in words I couldn't understand. Helga, herself, could drop into Swedish if it seemed worth her while to join in such conversations.

"It's nothing. I'll teach you," she had promised. But her enthusiasm had waned after a few attempts. So Helga became my interpreter as well as my most intimate friend. Without her, I should never have known the old men and women in the red brick house who were our hosts that night. I should never have seen Pastor Hanson bending over the melodeon or heard old Christine Berglund tell about the star.

Until we came to live at Fallen Leaf Lake, I had never seen so many old people together under one roof. There were rosy, fat old men and women; others frail and shrunken, and some with the limp look of tallow candles in hot weather.

It wasn't long before I knew them all by name. The spryer old men worked in the vegetable garden in summer, where Helga and I sometimes helped them pick berries or tomatoes until we were no longer hungry. Often we sat on the shady back porch and helped the old women shell peas, and then we would be rewarded by cookies or a tune from an old music box.

One tune in particular always made me feel sad and happy in an altogether satisfying way. *Butterflies at Haga,* they called it, and whether there happened to be two or a dozen listeners, old voices would chirp along with the music like crickets clinging fast to summer on a frosty night. Helga would join in, too, for she had learned it from her grandmother.

She tried to tell me what the words meant—something about a butterfly at a place called Haga, a butterfly hunting for a shelter from frost. Helga assured me that the butterfly didn't die; that it found a flowery parlor deep in some blossoms. She couldn't explain the rest of the song, but she thought the one who wrote it was homesick for the flowers and streams and woods of that place. I thought that must be true, because the old people often wiped their glasses after the music box stopped playing or sat very still with that look that meant they might be sitting close beside you but they were somewhere else in their minds.

"Now," Helga whispered when we reached the yard, "let's set the basket on the steps and get as close to the windows as we can."

The shades were not drawn. We could see those grouped about the polished nickel stove with rosy windows of isinglass, and others busy about the long table in the dining room. But they could not see us, creeping close, for we belonged to the darkness and the wind that worried the branches of two big hemlocks by the gate. We sang our carol, and it was like a play to watch the heads lift and the old faces come close to the windowpanes, with potted geraniums and begonias bright between us and them.

> *"Shine out, O Blessed Star,*
> *Promise of the dawn;*
> *Glad tidings send afar,*
> *Christ the Lord is born."*

Helga's voice soared so high it seemed to mount straight and unhindered as smoke from chimneys on winter mornings. My own voice took on unexpected power as I stood beside her singing.

"Merry Christmas!" we called even before the door was thrown open and the spiciness of cooking food came out to us as from the gates of heaven.

"Merry Christmas! *Göd Jul!*" Old voices hailed us, and hands drew us across the threshold into a world that had been transplanted across miles of salt sea and rolling, plowed land.

"Come; supper is ready." Pastor Hanson's chubby wife came bustling from the kitchen to take the basket we had brought.

Captain Christiansen took me by the hand, and I felt proud, because he looked so handsome in his blue coat with the brass buttons that he used to wear when he had his freight boat on Lake Superior.

There were sixteen of us, counting Helga and me, round that table with its white cloth, and its soup tureen at one end and round yellow cheese at the other. We all stood at our places while Pastor Hanson said a blessing in Swedish.

"There is a church in every man's heart," I remember he said in English at the end of his prayer, "but let us be sure that it is always God who preaches the sermon."

The smell from those bowls of pea soup stays with me yet! Golden and smooth and rich to the last spoonful, we ate it with slices of fresh rye bread and home-churned butter. Pastor Hanson, himself, sliced the cheese with a knife that shaved it into one yellow curl after another. Cinnamon and coffee and hot bread and molasses mingled in one delicious scent as dishes and cups and plates passed from hand to hand.

At last we gathered in the parlor and another scuttle of coal went into the big stove. The time had come for decorating the tree, and everyone took a hand in it except old Mrs. Berglund, who stayed in a wheelchair because of her rheumatism. But even she gave advice about where more strings of popcorn were needed and if the candles were placed where they would show best among the green branches. Mr. Johnson had made birds out of pinecones, and there were cranberries in long strings as red as the popcorn was white. There were hearts and crescents of tinfoil and balls made out of bright bits of worsted. But there was no star anywhere, and I wondered about that, for no Christmas tree could be complete without a star to light its tip. But I need not have been troubled about that, as it turned out.

The clock with the rising sun painted on its face struck eight, and the last candle was in its place. Pastor Hanson went over to the melodeon against the wall and began to play a Christmas carol. His plump fingers ran over the keys like pink mice, and he bent so lovingly to the music that there wasn't a single wrinkle in his neat black coat. He sang first in his deep, strong voice, and all the other voices came in on the chorus. I sang, too, English words along with their Swedish and Norwegian.

When we had finished, someone went over and whispered to old Mrs. Berglund in her wheelchair. From under her shawl she took out a small box that she held fast in her hands, which were thin and crooked as apple twigs. It was very still in the room for a moment, the kind of stillness that makes you know something exceedingly important is going to happen.

"Well, Pastor Hanson," she said, and held out the little box, "I did not think God would spare me for another year, but here I am, and here is the Christmas star."

"You must tell the children," he said. "It is right that they should hear before we hang it on the tree."

Helga and I pressed closer to the wheelchair. Her eyes were on our faces, yet they looked past us, as if she were summoning her own youth back from across the sea. The room was warm with the fire and our own breath. Even the tree standing in its load of loveliness gave out a woody fragrance, as if it, too, were breathing and listening with us.

"Yust like tonight it vas," Christine Berglund began, and I felt grateful that she was telling it so for my sake, even though her *j*s and *y*s and *v*s and *u*s had a way of changing places as she said them. "I vere eleven year old then and sick in my heart because Christmas is coming and I am so far from my mother and my brothers and sisters—"

I could see that big country estate as she told us about it—the stone walls and courtyard; the park with its thick woods; the tiled floors and great fireplaces; the heavy, carved furniture; the enormous beds that would have held her whole family of brothers and sisters. She was young to be sent away into service, and everything and everyone in that house was old, from the mistress to the servants who had tended her for many years.

"They had need of my young knees and quick fingers," she explained, "for they had grown too stiff to bend and dust under all the tables and chairs."

Christine had not minded the hard work. It was the stillness that made her sad. Some of those old servants were deaf, and those who were not had taken on the habit of silence from their mistress.

Sometimes she went with one of the servants to a certain room that was always kept locked. It was a beautiful room with painted furniture and colorful pictures and books. The bedspread was embroidered with spring flowers, but you could tell no one had slept there for years. Gilded cages hung empty, with no sweet-singing birds on their perches. The porcelain clock on the mantel was silent, as if time had stopped forever in that room. Whenever she went there with her dust cloths and brushes, Christine wondered who had slept in that bed and fed the birds that once had sung in the cages. She could get no answer from the servants, but at last she found out from Pastor Lange.

He came once each month to hold a service in the stone chapel, because his parish church was too far away for the servants to attend. Pastor Lange was a very kind old man, and Christine did not feel so lonely on the days when he came. He always spent the night there; though the mistress of the house never went into the chapel, after the service was over she sent for him, and they ate supper together and talked before the fire until bedtime. Christine knew this because once she was sent with a tray from the kitchen to set before them.

"God bless you, my child," Pastor Lange had said. "May you rest well."

But the old lady had kept her lips shut in a thin line, and she would not let her eyes rest on her young serving maid. It was the next morning that Pastor Lange answered Christine's questions. Their mistress had hardened her heart against every living thing because years ago she had lost her only child, a daughter as good as she was joyful and beautiful. When death had taken her child, the mother had turned as cold and gray as a boulder. She had ordered the girl's room closed and the birds let out of their cages. She had had a cloth hung over her portrait and every reminder of her presence taken from each nook and corner. Worst of all, she had summoned Pastor Lange and told him that she would live if she must, but he need never look for her in the family pew again. God had forsaken her, and Sunday and Easter and Christmas would be for her as any other days.

And she had kept her vow, though Pastor Lange had never ceased to pray that a miracle might turn her bitterness into faith once more.

"And did it?" Helga and I interrupted in our impatience.

But the story could not be hurried.

"Christmas, it is the vorst," old Christine went on, "for in that big house there is not one cake baked or one bit of green hung on any door. At home ve are poor, but ve put out grain for the birds and have our candles to light and our songs to sing."

Each night she cried as the holiday drew near. She thought of her mother and brothers and sisters all together in a house that was small but savory with holiday cooking. She thought also of the little church on Christmas Eve, with its lighted windows, and the graves outside, each with a torch set there to burn through the long hours till Christmas morning. It was right, her mother had told her, that even the dead should join with the living on the Holy Night. And there was nothing that Christine could do, a half-grown girl in that house of silence and old, old people, to show that Christmas was in her heart.

But once she had noticed near the chapel some tilted grave-stones and among them one not so old and gray as the others. Lichens covered the letters cut upon it. She was afraid to scrape away the moss to read the name, but there could be no harm, she thought, in putting a branch of green upon it. Perhaps she might

even take her own candle out there to burn and say a prayer and
sing a carol. The thought of that made her feel less lonely. She
hummed a Christmas hymn as she went back to her work, and it
was as she crossed the courtyard that something bright caught her
eye in a crack between two flagstones. She bent to pick it up and
there, half hidden by moss, was a pin, star-shaped and shining and
giving out jets of color as she turned it in the sun.

Like the Star of Bethlehem, she thought, and her heart beat fast
under the apron she wore, for surely it seemed like a sign to
comfort her.

She pinned it where no one would see it under her dress, and
all day she felt it close to her heart as she went about her duties.
That night she slept with it beneath her pillow, and she thought
of the Wise Men of old who had seen that other star in the East
and followed it to Bethlehem.

Next day she slipped out and stopped by the gravestones. On
the smallest stone she set a green branch of fir with cones. It
stood straight and fine—almost, Christine Berglund told us, like
the Christmas tree we had just trimmed.

"That night is Christmas Eve," she went on, "and I think there
can be no harm if I go out after it is dark and light my candle and
set the star there to keep vatch till it is morning."

But as the afternoon passed and twilight came, Christine did
not feel so happy. The hidden star pricked her with its points,
almost as if it were her own conscience telling her that stars were
not meant to be hidden, that what we pick up is not ours merely
for the finding. She tried to tell herself that it would be different
if she had found her treasure in the house, not out there between
the stones of the courtyard.

So darkness fell, and it was Christmas Eve. Some of the old
servants remembered and spoke of other times when there had

been laughter and festivity in those rooms, and the chapel bell ringing to call them to midnight service. Christine sat quiet until she could slip away to her little room. It was chilly there in the darkness because she dared not waste her candle.

At last the fires were banked and the house grew silent. Then Christine put on her cloak and crept down the stairs. She let herself into the courtyard, where nothing stirred but the shadows of trees beyond the walls. The moon was high above the stone turrets. She and it seemed to be the only things that moved in that world of winter quiet. She passed the chapel where no bells pealed from the dark belfry. There were the old tilted gravestones and the one with the bit of green to mark it. Her fingers shook as she set her candle on the headstone and tried to light it. Twice it went out before the small flame shone clear. Her hand still trembled as she took out the star and pinned it among the green needles of the fir bough.

"And then I get down on my knees and first I say 'Our Father.' Then I make another one that is mine, so God shall know that I do not forget the night of our Savior's birth. It is hard for me to find the words for my prayer, and my teeth are chattering like little hammers, so I don't hear someone come tap-tapping on the stones—"

"Oh!" Helga and I drew sharp breaths. "Who was it?"

But old Christine must tell the story in her own way.

"There I am on my knees," she repeated, "praying to God; and my candle is still burning. Yes, that is how she found me."

We dared not interrupt her again, but our eyes never left her face.

"'Mistress,' I said," she went on, "'forgive me.' But she don't answer me; she yust stand there and look at the stone and the candle."

"And then what?" We whispered the question.

"Oh, I am so afraid I cry, and I give her back the pin, and she yust stand there and turn it in her hands, and she act like she is seeing a ghost."

They must have stood so a long time. The candle burned out on the headstone before the old mistress took Christine back to the house. She did not speak until they reached the great hall, though tears ran down her cheeks at each step they took. Her hands reached for the bell rope, and the house echoed to her frantic ringing. Christine could hear the servants hurrying to and fro upstairs in answer to the summons.

"I think she send for them because I have done a bad thing," old Christine told us, "so I stand and shiver there and don't know what is going to happen to me. And then they come down, all so sleepy they forget to make their curtsies. And Mistress point to me, and I cry so I don't see her face anymore. But she say to them, 'Go; make a fire in the locked room. Spread linen and blankets on the bed and warm it, and bring food, that this child may eat and be comforted.'

"I think I don't hear her right, but they take me there, and I see the fire lighted and the bed vaiting, so I don't try to think anymore. I yust lie down with the flowers spread over me, and I sleep and sleep. And there is no one to come and shake me at sunrise to help in the kitchen. I vake, and it is Christmas morning and bells are ringing so sveet I think I dream them from home. But they are ringing in the chapel. Then the maids come and bring me a beautiful varm dress that smells of cloves and lavender. And they dress me in it, and I ask them the meaning of all this; but they yust smile and say, 'Pastor Lange, he vill tell you.'"

And, sure enough, Pastor Lange and the old mistress came from the chapel. He had driven since sunrise in the carriage she had sent to bring him there.

"You shall see for yourself, Pastor," the old coachman had said, "that the day of miracles is not past."

So Christine went down to meet them in the dress that was heavy with gold embroidery and slippers so soft she seemed to be walking on snow. These rooms were no longer gray and gloomy but warm with leaping fires. The covers were gone from the portrait of a laughing girl no older than she. Her dress was the same that Christine wore, and the star showed plainly on the painted folds. Christine marveled at each change she saw about her, most of all at her mistress's face, which was still sad, but no longer set like stone.

Then Pastor Lange put his hand on Christine's head and blessed her in God's name. But to the old woman he said, "Blessed are they that mourn, for they shall be comforted."

And Christine sat between them at dinner, and felt strange that she should now be served who had so lately carried in the dishes.

"And after dinner is over Pastor Lange he tells me that it is indeed a miracle God has vorked through me to bring faith to our mistress. I don't understand how that can be, for it was not right that I keep the pin and tell no one. But Pastor Lange does not know how to explain that to me. So he says, 'Christine, it must have been that God vas in your heart to do this thing.' 'No, Pastor,' I tell him the truth; 'it vas Christmas in my heart.' And Pastor Lange he don't scold me, he yust say maybe that is the same thing."

Old Christine was growing tired. Her voice had dwindled to a thin thread of sound by the time she had answered our questions. . . . Yes, the pin had belonged to her mistress's daughter. She had lost it one winter day and grown so chill hunting for it in the courtyard that she had fallen ill and died. It was her gravestone by the chapel that Christine had chosen to light and decorate with green. So great had been that mother's grief that it was more than thirty years since she had spoken her daughter's name or let anything be a reminder. But Christine's candle shining on Christmas Eve had been like a sign sent from her dead child by a living one on that most happy night of the year.

So Christine no longer served as a maid in that great house. She lived as the old woman's daughter, and in winter the rooms were warm and bright with fires and laughter, and in summer sweet with flowers and the singing of birds.

"And see, here is the star to hang on the tree."

"The same one? The very same?"

"Yes, the same. It goes vith me always since that night."

We touched the five shining points with wonder in our finger-tips before Christine's old fingers lifted it from the bed of cotton.

"Real diamonds and not one missing," she said proudly as she handed it to Captain Christiansen, because he was tall enough to set it on the topmost tip. "But I never think it vould come all the vay to America. I never think I come all that vay myself."

We watched it send out little jets of brightness when the candles were lighted below and all the old faces shining in loveliest of light. We sang another carol all together, and then it was time to go home with Helga's father, who had come for us.

"Good night." Their voices followed us to the door. *"Göd Jul!* Merry Christmas!"

"Merry Christmas!" Helga and I called back before we turned to follow her father's lantern into the wintry dark.

Rachel Field
1894–1942

Novelist, poet, playwright, and editor, Field was one of the most beloved family writers of her time; among her best known works are *Calico Bush, Time Out of Mind, All This and Heaven Too, And Now Tomorrow,* and her continuing best-seller, *A Prayer for a Child.*

Raymond Macdonald Alden

WHY THE
CHIMES RANG

I *first heard this story . . . oh . . . more years ago than I care to admit. I have cherished it all through the years. There are many variant texts of this plot, written by a number of authors, all based on several of our Lord's parables; but this is one of the more special ones.*

For a number of years now, it has gradually, like cream, been rising to the top. And, in recent years and months, several Christmas story aficionados have asked me to give it serious consideration for inclusion. As I always do, I continually solicit the Lord's guidance as to which stories to include; and I am convicted that this old story ought to be in our eighth collection.

There was once, in a faraway country where few people have ever traveled, a wonderful church. It stood on a high hill in the midst of a great city; and every Sunday, as well as on sacred days like Christmas, thousands of people climbed the hill to its great archways, looking like lines of ants all moving in the same direction.

When you came to the building itself, you found stone columns and dark passages, and a grand entrance leading to the main room of the church. This room was so long that one standing at the doorway could scarcely see to the other end, where the choir stood by the marble altar. In the farthest corner was the organ; and this organ was so loud, that sometimes when it played, the people for miles around would close their shutters and prepare for a great thunderstorm. Altogether, no such church as this was ever seen before, especially when it lighted up for some festival and crowded with people, young and old.

But the strangest thing about the whole building was the wonderful chime of bells. At one corner of the church was a great gray tower, with ivy growing over it as far up as one could see. I say as far as one could see, because the tower was quite great enough to fit the great church, and it rose so far into the sky that it was only in very fair weather that anyone claimed to be able to see the top. Even then one could not be certain that it was in sight. Up and up and up climbed the stones and the ivy; and, as the men who built the church had been dead for hundreds of years, every one had forgotten how high the tower was supposed to be.

Now all the people knew that at the top of the tower was a chime of Christmas bells. They had hung there ever since the church had been built, and were the most beautiful bells in the world. Some thought it was because a great musician had cast them and arranged them in their place; others said it was because of the great height, which reached up where the air was clearest and purest: However that might be, no one who had ever heard the chimes denied that they were the sweetest in the world. Some described them as sounding like angels far up in the sky; others, as sounding like strange winds singing through the trees.

But the fact was that no one had heard them for years and years. There was an old man living not far from the church, who said that his mother had spoken of hearing them when she was a little girl, and he was the only one who was sure of as much as that. They were Christmas chimes, you see, and were not meant to be played by men or on common days. It was the custom on Christmas Eve for all the people to bring to the church their offerings to the Christ child; and when the greatest and best offering was laid on the altar, there used to come sounding through the music of the choir the Christmas chimes far up in the tower. Some said that the wind rang them, and others that they were so high that the angels could set them swinging. But for many long years they had never been heard.

It was said that people had been growing less careful of their gifts for the Christ child, and that no offering was brought great enough to deserve the music of the chimes. Every Christmas Eve the rich people still crowded to the altar, each one trying to bring some better gift than any other, without giving anything that he wanted for himself, and the church was crowded with those who thought that perhaps the wonderful bells might be heard again. But although the service was splendid and the offerings plenty, only the roar of the wind could be heard far up in the stone tower.

Now a number of miles from the city, in a little country village where nothing could be seen of the great church but glimpses of

the tower when the weather was fine, lived a boy named Pedro
and his little brother. They knew very little about the Christmas
chimes, but they had heard of the service in the church on
Christmas Eve and had a secret plan, which they had often talked
over when by themselves, to go see the beautiful celebration.

"Nobody can guess, Little Brother," Pedro would say, "all the
fine things there are to see and hear; and I have heard it said that
the Christ child sometimes comes down to bless the service.
What if we could see Him?"

The day before Christmas was bitterly cold, with a few lonely
snowflakes flying in the air and a hard white crust on the ground.
Sure enough, Pedro and Little Brother were able to slip quietly
away early in the afternoon; and although the walking was hard
in the frosty air, before nightfall they had trudged so far, hand in
hand, that they saw the lights of the big city just ahead of them.
Indeed, they were about to enter one of the great gates in the
wall that surrounded it when they saw something dark on the
snow near their path and stepped aside to look at it.

It was a poor woman who had fallen just outside the city, too
sick and tired to get in where she might have found shelter. The
soft snow made of a drift a sort of pillow for her, and she would
soon be so sound asleep in the wintry air that no one could ever
waken her again. All this Pedro saw in a moment, and he knelt
down beside her and tried to rouse her, even tugging at her arm
a little, as though he would have tried to carry her away. He
turned her face toward him so that he could rub some of the
snow on it, and when he had looked at her silently a moment he
stood up again, and said: "It's no use, Little Brother. You will
have to go on alone."

"Alone?" cried Little Brother. "And you not see the Christmas
festival?"

"No," said Pedro, and he could not keep back a bit of a chok-
ing sound in his throat. "See this poor woman? Her face looks

like the Madonna in the chapel window, and she will freeze to death if nobody cares for her. Everyone has gone to the church now, but when you come back you can bring someone to help her. I will rub her to keep her from freezing and perhaps get her to eat the bun that is left in my pocket."

"But I can not bear to leave you and go on alone," said Little Brother.

"Both of us need not miss the service," said Pedro, "and it had better be I than you. You can easily find your way to the church; and you must see and hear everything twice, Little Brother— once for you and once for me. I am sure the Christ child must know how I should love to come with you and worship Him; and oh! if you get a chance, Little Brother, to slip up to the altar without getting in anyone's way, take this little silver piece of mine, and lay it down for my offering when no one is looking. Do not forget where you have left me, and forgive me for not going with you."

In this way he hurried Little Brother off to the city, and winked hard to keep back the tears as he heard the crunching footsteps sounding farther and farther away in the twilight. It was pretty hard to lose the music and splendor of the Christmas celebration that he had been planning for so long, and spend the time instead in that lonely place in the snow.

The great church was a wonderful place that night. Everyone said that it had never looked so bright and beautiful before. When the organ played and the thousands of people sang, the walls shook with the sound, and little Pedro, away outside the city wall, felt the earth tremble around him.

At the close of the service came the procession with the offerings to be laid on the altar. Rich men and great men marched proudly up to lay down their gifts to the Christ child. Some brought wonderful jewels, some baskets of gold so heavy that they could scarcely carry them down the aisle. A great writer laid down a book that he had been writing for years and years. And last of all walked the king of the country, hoping with all the rest to win for himself the chime of the Christmas bells. There went a great murmur through the church, as the people saw the king take from his head the royal crown, all set with precious stones, and lay it gleaming on the altar, as his offering to the holy Child. "Surely," everyone said, "we shall hear the bells now, for nothing like this has ever happened before."

But still only the cold old wind was heard in the tower, and the people shook their heads; and some of them said, as they had before, that they never really believed the story of the chimes and doubted if they ever rang at all.

The procession was over, and the choir began the closing hymn. Suddenly the organist stopped playing as though he had been shot, and everyone looked at the old minister, who was standing by the altar holding up his hand for silence. Not a sound could be heard from anyone in the church, but as all the people strained their ears to listen, there came softly, but distinctly, swinging through the air, the sound of the chimes in the tower. So far away, and yet so clear the music seemed—so much sweeter were the notes than anything that had been heard before, rising and falling away up there in the sky, that the people in the church sat for a moment as still as though something held each of them by the shoulders. Then they all stood up together and stared straight at the altar to see what great gift had awakened the long-silent bells.

But all that the nearest of them saw was the childish figure of Little Brother, who had crept softly down the aisle when no one was looking and had laid Pedro's little piece of silver on the altar.

Raymond M. Alden
1 8 7 3 – 1 9 2 4

Besides this story, Alden, a New Hartford, New York, educator, also wrote and published such works as *Shakespeare, An Introduction to Poetry,* and *Knights of the Silver Shield.*

Edward H. Imme

MERRY CHRISTMAS, MRS. MARIGOLD

For twelve long years Mr. Moseler and Mr. Crump, although living next to each other in the same house, had greeted each other with only grunts and growls. Not even Christmas thawed the icy curtain between them—until the fruitcakes didn't arrive.

It was Christmas Eve. The snow had begun to fall down lightly, dancing in little whirls around the corners of the buildings and swarming like clouds of white moths in the yellow glow of the streetlamps, when Mr. Moseler and Mr. Crump met at Schulz's Café for their evening meal.

Their meeting was neither accidental nor planned but was the inevitable result of the fixed pattern of their lives which, by the calcifying processes of habit, bus schedules, and advancing age, had settled into hard, unvarying grooves.

Schulz's Café happened to be that point at which those grooves intersected without fail, each working day at 6:10 P.M.

Mr. Moseler greeted Mr. Crump with a grunt to which that individual replied with a disinterested nod. This had become standard ritual with them before partaking of their evening meal.

Big Schulz's smile was especially broad that evening, his face a glistening sun with a stubble of prickly black beard.

"Merry Christmas!" beamed Big Schulz.

Mr. Moseler extended his arm along the counter in the direction of a folded copy of the evening paper.

Mr. Crump said, "It's a lousy Christmas!"

Big Schulz was not altogether taken aback by this reply for, having seen these two grumble their way through twelve Christmases running, he half expected something of the sort. He was, nevertheless, indignant.

"Look!" he said. "There ain't no such thing! Ain't no such thing as a lousy Christmas."

"Hmp!" grunted Mr. Crump. "Who you trying to kid? Once a year everybody runs around yelling, 'Merry Christmas! Merry Christmas!' And then everybody else is supposed to feel real fine. Makes me tired, that's what!" And he rubbed his dry hands across his chin.

Big Schulz was getting angry. "A-a-rh! You sour old apples

oughta be ashamed," he said. "You should be cheerful at Christmastime."

"Why?" demanded Mr. Crump, at which Mr. Moseler peered sharply across the top of the evening paper at Big Schulz.

Big Schulz didn't tell them why. Mainly because he could not, for the moment, think of just why it should be that way. All he knew was that he was excited to close shop and go home because the children were in the Christmas program over at the church, and Dolly was going to say her first Christmas recitation, and after the service there would be the presents around the Christmas tree at home, and Louis and Lena were coming over with their kids, and altogether it promised to be a fine evening. But all this was too much to put into just one simple *why,* so he just said, "Don't you know what Christmas is?"

"Sure I know what Christmas is," said Mr. Moseler like a terrier taking out after the neighbor's cat. "Christmas is a promotion scheme. The biggest promotion scheme ever invented to get suckers to spend their money on a lot of foolishness. Now how about some service?"

"I got Christmas Eve Special tonight. Turkey, mashed po—"

"See what I mean?" Mr. Moseler giggled in triumph. "Christmas Special! All over town. It's just a promotion, and you yourself got to admit it, Schulz. Make mine the usual."

"Mine too," said Mr. Crump.

"Ham 'n' eggs 'n' fried potatoes!" grumbled Big Schulz back in the kitchen. "For twelve solid years! What a pair!"

From Schulz's Café the Crump groove and the Moseler groove paralleled each other, not of choice but of necessity, to a large house that stared with a gray and emotionless face across a nubble-choked old hedge at the corner of the block.

Once it had been a sumptuous home whose rooms had known

the sounds of gaiety and affection, but through many downward twists of fortune, it had come at last to serve out its remaining years as a rooming house kept by a drab and perpetually weary-looking little woman with the inappropriately bright-sounding name of Mrs. Helen Marigold.

The house had two front doors.

One door entered directly into the living room of Mrs. Marigold's ground floor apartments and was used exclusively by herself. The other provided entrance to a gloomy hallway that extended back to rooms 2 and 3 and with a stairway to the upper floor, where lived the gentlemen Crump and Moseler in rooms 5 and 7 respectively.

Immediately to the right upon entering this tenant's doorway was a glassed door, which permitted access from the hall as well as a view into Mrs. Marigold's living room.

Approaching the house, the two men noted that it was entirely darkened except for the dim yellow light in Mrs. Marigold's living room.

"Guess everybody's out tonight except the Old Lady," said Mr. Moseler.

"I turned down an invitation myself," said Mr. Crump. "Didn't feel so good today. Thought I'd turn in early."

Invitation! Hah! You old hypocrite, thought Mr. Moseler in a tight little corner of his mind. But to Mr. Crump he said, "Well, the Old Lady's home anyway."

"Isn't she always?" reflected Mr. Crump.

After this exchange they ascended the stairs and went, each to his own room and to his own thoughts and the enjoyment of them. Before entering their rooms, however, each paused curiously in front of the door and examined the floor, probing the dusky shadows with a foot as if in search of something, then went in and closed his door behind him.

Perhaps half an hour of peace ensued, during which time there was no sound from any quarter of the big house, which stood shrouded in musty shadows.

Then Mr. Moseler was startled by a rapping on his door.

"Who's there?" he cried.

"It's me. Crump."

"Well, what do you want?"

"Well, open the door."

Mr. Crump came in and surveyed the furnishings of Mr. Moseler's apartment with a critical eye. It was the first time he had ever been in it.

"Did you get a fruitcake?" he asked abruptly.

"Well, now that you mention it, no," said Mr. Moseler. "How about you?"

"Not that I care about it, understand, but I was just curious to know," said Mr. Crump.

"I suppose she just hasn't brought them up yet," ventured Mr. Moseler.

"Maybe so," said Mr. Crump. And after a bit he arose and returned to his room.

Left to himself and the musty silence, Mr. Moseler began to feel strangely uneasy.

At first it was the absence of the fruitcake that troubled him. In all the twelve years that he had lived in this house Mrs. Marigold had never failed to place a brightly done-up little fruitcake in front of each tenant's door on Christmas Eve. Yet here it was Christmas Eve, and no fruitcake. It troubled him.

———————————————————————

The other thing that troubled him even more was the fact that the absence of Mrs. Marigold's Christmas fruitcake should trouble him so. It had never seemed important before. In fact, he had been a little annoyed by them, and Crump and he had both affected a certain disdain at such frivolity. Yet here he was, not only wondering why he hadn't gotten a fruitcake this year but actually troubled about it in a strange way. And then there was that business of Crump pounding on his door to ask if he had gotten his fruitcake yet. He couldn't brush the webs of it from his mind and found himself listening inadvertently for sounds from Mrs. Marigold's apartments below. But the house remained silent.

Mr. Moseler wondered if the other tenants had received their fruitcakes yet. If so, why should he and Crump have been overlooked? And then he remembered that, after all, he had never bothered to give Mrs. Marigold anything, never sent her a card, nor—and this gave him a genuine pang—could he recall having ever thanked her for her little gift. Not that it was important, of course, yet it gave him a strange, uneasy feeling. It was as though a last tiny candle went out leaving the room in heavy darkness, and one suddenly realized how very dark is dark and how light is even a tiny light.

This is a foolish way for me to feel, he thought. *Perhaps a walk to the drugstore will clear this thing from my mind,* and he began to put on his overcoat and his rubbers.

Meanwhile Mr. Crump, after retiring to his room, had been experiencing much the same emotions. So it was that when Mr. Moseler left his room and walked down the gloomy hallway and descended the stairs, there, at the bottom of the stairs, was Mr. Crump. He, too, was about to go out but had paused for a moment to peer through the glass door into Mrs. Marigold's living room.

"For heaven's sake, Crump! What are you doing?"

"Oh! I-uh was about to go for a walk," explained Mr. Crump. Then, after a moment, he added, "I suppose she's gone out for the evening. Don't you suppose?"

Mr. Moseler thought about this, and it seemed quite a logical explanation except that, in all the time that he had known her, Mrs. Marigold had never gone out of an evening. He mentioned this to Mr. Crump, who was compelled to agree.

They stood for a moment peering through the glass. Something seemed not quite right about the living room. Mr. Crump was the first to define it.

"Look!" he exclaimed. "The Christmas tree."

Mr. Moseler looked. He glanced quickly sidewise at Mr. Crump, then looked again. Finally he said, "What are you talking about? I don't see any Christmas tree."

"That's just it," said Mr. Crump. "There isn't any. But she's *always* had one! A little one sitting on that small table in the corner. Remember? No fruitcake. No Christmas tree. Do you suppose Mrs. Marigold is sick?"

A sense of trouble pierced Mr. Moseler like a draft of cold air through the dark hall. But he quickly shook it off.

"Pshaw!" he replied. "She's just come to her senses, that's all. Anyway, if she were going out for Christmas Eve, why should she bother with a tree? You're worse than an old woman, Crump."

With that he opened the outside door and stepped out onto the porch, where he stood for a moment in the chill air. He pulled the collar of his coat up around his cheeks and happened to glance at the porch in front of Mrs. Marigold's entrance. For a long while he stood thus as though struggling to rid himself of some thought that kept tugging at his mind. The house behind him lay shrouded in deathlike silence, and the snow lay deep and white and undisturbed on Mrs. Marigold's front porch. He went back into the hallway and drew the door shut.

"She's in there," said Mr. Moseler.

"Moseler," said Mr. Crump, "I'm worried." He knocked on the door. There was no response. "I think we should go in," he said.

So Mr. Moseler and Mr. Crump found themselves in Mrs. Marigold's living quarters on Christmas Eve and were greeted there by the same complete and utter silence that pervaded the whole house.

They moved uncertainly through the living room and the dining room.

In the dining room they found an old piano.

"That's odd," said Mr. Moseler, "I have never heard Mrs. Marigold play the piano."

On top of the piano, at one end, was a photograph of a man, taken many years before. Across it was written the name "Alvin."

"This must have been her husband," said Mr. Crump.

"Been dead a long time," said Mr. Moseler.

There was some sheet music spread out on the piano as though the old, yellowed sheets were waiting for their melodies. It was simple music, written for a child.

Opposite the man's picture on the piano was a photograph of a lovely young girl of perhaps ten years of age, and tucked into a corner of the paper frame was a tiny snapshot of a new grave heaped with floral pieces.

The two men returned to the living room. There was still one door, standing slightly ajar, which they had both pointedly ignored. It was the door to Mrs. Marigold's bedroom.

"Listen!" whispered Mr. Crump. "Did you hear something?"

They stood without breathing, and in the cold silence there was a sound; faint, unrecognizable. It came from beyond the door they dreaded to enter.

Mr. Crump shuddered and then squared himself with duty and pushed into the room. Moseler followed, and they fumbled for a light switch on the wall. With a click the revealing light came on.

A man's old-fashioned watch on a heavy gold chain hung from the head of the bed, and it was ticking, ticking, ticking, so close that it almost touched the cheek of Mrs. Helen Marigold. An old black pipe lay on the small stand beside the bed together with a glass and an empty bottle. A child's doll lay on the pillow beside her head.

They looked from the woman lying on the bed to the empty bottle on the table, and the thought came at first reluctantly, then broke over them like a crash of thunder.

"She's taken poison!"

"She's still alive, though!"

"I'll call a doctor!"

"Hurry, man! I'll see if I can rouse her."

So they brought the night alive, and the doctor came in a screaming ambulance and worked with her.

"I think we can save her," said the doctor. "Thank God you came when you did."

Mrs. Marigold stirred and her eyes fluttered, and Mr. Crump and Mr. Moseler stood miserably beside the bed.

"Al?" she asked in a sweet, tired voice.

"No, Mrs. Marigold. It isn't Al. It's just us. Crump and Moseler."

"Al, honey?" persisted the sweet, tired voice.

The doctor ushered them out to the living room. "We'll rush her to the hospital," he said. "I think she'll be all right."

Crump and Moseler looked at each other and at the doctor.

"But why would she . . . ," Mr. Moseler began.

"I guess she just couldn't take it any longer," said the doctor.

"Well," said Mr. Crump, "keeping a place like this and as neat as she does is just too much work for one poor old woman like that."

The doctor saw that Mrs. Marigold was placed comfortably on the stretcher. "There, now," he said soothingly. "Everything's going to be all right." Then he turned to the two men.

"It wasn't the work," he said. "It was the loneliness."

———————————————

The next day being Christmas Day, Crump and Moseler went to the hospital to see how Mrs. Marigold was getting on. They looked odd with their arms full of packages they had bought at the drugstore that stayed open on Christmas Day for emergencies, and they were quite embarrassed with it all, but there was a new light in their eyes.

Mrs. Marigold was embarrassed, too. "Oh, it was so kind of you to come," she said. "So kind of you. And it was such a foolish thing for me to do. So very, very foolish. I don't know why. I just don't know. How did you ever come in to find me? God must have sent you. Yes, that's it. God must have sent you."

"Well," said Mr. Moseler, "I guess He did. We missed your fruitcakes, and we got to thinking."

"We brought you a few presents," said Mr. Crump.

They laid their gifts on Mrs. Marigold's bed, and then they unwrapped a bulkier package and began to lay out the pieces it contained. They placed them on a clean, white cloth on a little table beside her bed. Some shepherds, tiny animals, Joseph and Mary and a little manger, and Wise Men kneeling.

"A crèche!" exclaimed Mrs. Marigold, and she sounded almost like a child. She took the manger in her frail hands. There was the figure of a tiny baby inside. A sweet expression softened the lines of her face.

"The Christ child!" she said softly, as if remembering something from long ago. "I guess I just forgot. I guess I just plumb forgot."

"We're the ones that forgot, Mrs. Marigold," said Mr. Crump.

Mr. Moseler agreed with this, and while they were standing beside her bed looking at the figures in the Christmas scene, a quiet peace came over their hearts like the soft touch of an angel's wing.

On their way home they stopped at Schulz's Café for dinner.

"Merry Christmas, Schulz!" cried Mr. Crump.

"We'll have the Christmas Dinner Special with all the trimmings!" said Mr. Moseler.

Wendy Miller

FEELS GOOD
IN MY HEART

***

This is a first: the first Christmas in My Heart *story*
to be spawned by an earlier Christmas in My Heart
story. For good measure, it was written by the author of
one of the most beloved stories we have ever published,
"Charlie's Blanket."

On the surface, it is all about "The Trading Game,"
but deep down it is about more, much *more, than just*
a game.

"Mom, where's your new book?" Amanda asked as she ran her fingers along the books in the shelf.

"Beth was reading it," her mother answered.

"Beth," Amanda hollered at her sister. "Where's Mom's new book?"

Beth shrugged. "Brian had it after me."

"Brian!" both sisters yelled together.

Brian came grinning into the room with a book tucked firmly under his arm. He obviously had heard the entire exchange and was more than pleased to be in possession of the book his sisters wanted. He was in a good bargaining position, and he knew it. As the youngest of the family, he rarely had controlling power in any situation.

"Did you call me?" he asked in a sweet and innocent voice.

"Yeah, I need this," Amanda said, reaching out to grab the book. Brian twisted away, keeping it out of her reach.

"I'm reading it right now. I just got started, and I want to read the whole thing. Every single story."

Amanda knew it would take days for Brian to read the whole book. She put her hands on her hips. "I want to read it now before we have to go to bed." She glared at him.

"Me, too," he shrugged nonchalantly.

His sister changed her tactics. Dropping down onto the couch she sighed, "OK, if you don't want me to read it to you . . ."

That did it. Quick as a wink, he was snuggled against her and opening the book to the last story. Beth came over to sit on the other side when Amanda began to read.

Wendy looked up from her needlework and smiled at the three huddled on the couch. Adam, her oldest, was sitting on a chair close by pretending to do his homework. He was too old to admit he was listening to the story and too interested to move away. The book was a collection of stories and had just come in the mail a few days ago. The last story was about a gift exchange taking place at

Christmas and was by far the children's favorite. The exchange was done as a game with the gifts being traded, exchanged and stolen from other family members. The children were so engrossed in the story that they felt as if they were there watching it all happen, and they laughed out loud as Amanda read. Even after the story was finished and the book was closed, the kids sat still while the story lingered in their minds. Finally Beth spoke.

"Mom, could we do that?"

"Do what, Bethy?"

"Do that exchange game at Christmas." All the kids looked eagerly at their mother. It was Adam who answered first.

"No, we can't. There are only six of us in the family, and there needs to be a lot more than that to make it really fun." His siblings were quiet for a moment while they considered this. Adam was always logical and practical and usually made a good point. They decided that he was right, but there might be another way: They could play the game when they got together with their dad's family. With the grandparents, aunts, uncles, and cousins, there would be seventeen.

"Seventeen is a good number, Adam. Don't you think so?" Brian wanted to convince his big brother.

"Seventeen is good, but it still won't work. It has to be the right people, too. It just won't work with them." He shook his head.

"What do you mean it has to be the right people?" Amanda demanded. "It doesn't matter who they are. You just don't want to do it, that's all."

"It does so matter, Amanda," he answered. "Can you imagine what would happen if you took a present away from one of the three little cousins? They would scream and cry and all the parents would be mad, and then we would get in trouble for making them cry and then we would be mad and then . . ."

". . . the whole thing would be wrecked," finished Amanda.

Beth and Brian nodded. Adam was right again. It had to be the right number and the right people, too.

Eventually it was decided that Grandma's would be the perfect place. Grandma was Wendy's mom. There was a total of thirteen when all of Wendy's family was gathered, and thirteen was almost as good as seventeen. The youngest cousin was ten, the same age as Brian, and they were all good sports and enjoyed playing just about anything. Adam approved the decision, and so did Wendy. The kids cheered and sat down to read the story all over again.

Wendy's thoughts were busy. The kids had thought things out fairly well, especially with Adam's guidance. However, they had overlooked one rather large problem. Her sister would not approve of spending money on gifts that might or might not end up in the hands of who she intended them for. Fun is fun, but money is money. The solution was for Wendy and her husband, Peter, to buy all the gifts themselves. They would buy thirteen small gifts. If all the gifts were small, it wouldn't really hurt the budget, and the children did want to try out the game. She talked it over with Peter, and he agreed.

For the next month, Wendy picked up little things. A pair of socks, a toy truck, some bracelets. A set of salt and pepper shakers in the shape of Santa and Mrs. Claus would be a hit for the three women, who all had a collection of salt and peppers. The gifts were carefully hidden from curious eyes.

The day before Christmas the family met at Grandma's house. There was much excitement over being together again. Exclamations over decorations and gifts and way too much good food. Nobody could cook like Grandma!

Finally the time came. Amanda explained the rules, and the game was started. It was everything they had hoped for. Gifts were snatched, traded, and wrestled for. The children squealed with delight. It had been the highlight of their Christmas. Peter and Wendy smiled as they watched the family. Who would have thought that it would have meant so much?

Christmas was barely over when Amanda reminded her mother to start picking up gifts for next year's exchange game. It was a good idea to start a year ahead of time. Wendy found a board game at a discount store. A ceramic angel candlestick was given away to the first twenty customers at the department store one day after Christmas. Slowly but surely the gifts began to pile up until there were enough.

As Christmas approached again, Peter's carpentry business slowed down, and money became short. They would still have a nice Christmas, but they would have to watch every penny. The only concern the children had was whether or not they would be able to play their exchange game again. Wendy assured them that the presents were already bought. Even something for their new baby cousin.

"I think you will be even more happy to know that the gifts this year are bigger and better than last year. I had a lot more time to find some good deals. It will be extra good," Wendy told them. She was almost knocked over as they all tried to hug her at the same time. The exchange game was so important to them: It was definitely becoming a tradition.

Just a week before Christmas, as they sat around the dinner table, Wendy told them of a family in town that was having problems. The husband had been out of work for a long time. The family had very little food and no money to buy gifts for the three children.

After hearing the story, Peter made a quick decision: "We just killed the turkeys. Let's take one and give it to them tomorrow."

The children all looked at each other and then down at their plates. How fortunate they were to have two loving parents, presents for Christmas, a big farm, and all the turkeys, chickens and other animals, as well as all the vegetables from Wendy's big garden. They were all thinking the same thought:

"Mom, don't they have a new baby?" Adam asked.

"Yes, they do," she answered.

"Didn't you buy a baby gift for the exchange?" he questioned.

"Yes, I did."

"Well, I think we should give them our exchange game gifts."

Wendy looked around the table at the other children. They were all nodding in agreement. Wendy left the table and returned carrying a big box. From it she pulled out a doll, two coffee mugs, the board game, the candleholder, some baby toys, colored pencils, and numerous other gifts. She wondered if they would change their minds when they saw all that they would be giving up.

"We can help you wrap them after supper is cleaned up, Mom," Amanda decided.

"I can stick the name tags and bows on them," Brian piped in.

"You could take them over when no one is home so they won't know who did it," Beth suggested. "That would make it even more fun."

And so they did. After supper they wrapped and tagged the gifts, discussing all the while how surprised and happy the family would be to find the gifts and the turkey on their doorstep. Not once did any of them mention the loss of their precious gift exchange. They went together to deliver the parcels. "This is what you really want to do?" Wendy asked them as they approached the house.

She could tell by the glow on their faces that Amanda spoke for them all: "Mom, we can always play the game next year. But for now, this feels good in my heart."

Tears came to Wendy's eyes as she marveled at the love and generosity of her children. It felt good in her heart, too.

Nancy N. Rue

A GIRL
LIKE ME

To Marijane, all the magic had gone out of Christmas—no, make that out of life. She was thirteen and in junior high, but where was all the excitement she had dreamed of?

And then there was that dweeb Jake Picard.

Nancy Rue's story, "The Red Envelope," was one of the hits of Christmas in My Heart, book 7. Nancy Rue, of Lebanon, Tennessee, is one of the top writers of Christian stories for young people in America today and is perhaps best known for her Christian Heritage historical fiction series copublished by Focus on the Family and Tyndale House.

MONDAY, DECEMBER 17, 7:00 P.M.
IN OUR LIVING ROOM

"OK, we've got Jeremy picking up the tree—"

"Check!" Jeremy said—and knocked a plate of Christmas cookies off the coffee table.

"Mom planning Christmas dinner—"

"Check," Mom said, dimples going in and out at light speed.

"Sara taking care of decorations—"

Pause.

Jeremy looked hard at her. "Well?" he said.

Sara rolled her eyes but laughed. "OK, OK—check," she said.

Dad looked back at the list. "Goodies for the shut-ins—that means everybody, whenever you have time to get in the kitchen and whip up a batch of something."

"Jeremy, please do not find time to get in the kitchen and whip up something," Sara said to my little brother. "We don't want these old people breaking their upper plates."

Jeremy stuck his tongue out at our older sister, but he still kept grinning. Nothing daunted the Christmas spirit of a ten-year-old. Now, a thirteen-year-old like me—nah, it didn't daunt mine either. I didn't have any to begin with.

"Mj," Dad said to me, dropping his eyes down the list, "we don't have you down for anything yet. What do you want to do?"

I shrugged. I'd been shrugging so much during the family meeting it was starting to look like a Jane Fonda shoulder exercise.

"You have to do *something*," Jeremy said.

"I do not!"

"Maybe Marijane hasn't thought of anything yet." Mom deepened a dimple at me, but I didn't smile back.

"Anyway," Dad said, "time's a-wasting for me to take each of you shopping for—" he shifted his eyes toward my mother and hissed loudly—"a present for You-Know-Who!"

Jeremy practically squirmed off the couch, and my mother grabbed the cookies before they took another dump.

"Dad, thanks," Sara said, "but I can go on my own this year."

Dad sighed. "I know when I've been usurped by a flock of giggling girls who take five hours to do one side of the mall." He looked at me. "You and me, Mj. Tomorrow night. We can do the *whole* mall in two hours."

Again I shrugged, but nobody noticed because Jeremy was launching into a ten-minute whine about how he wanted the first night's Mom-shopping. When the doorbell rang, I dashed for the foyer. Anything to get out of there.

Well, almost anything.

When I opened the door, all I saw were his eyes blinking from behind those oversized glasses. The rest of his face was covered by the notepad he was holding.

"Collecting for your newspaper subscription," Jake said, and then he looked up. "Oh, it's you!"

"Of course it's me. I live here."

He lowered his pad to reveal the smile that was too big for his face. He sniffed and let it ramble all the way up to his earlobes. "I smell cookies."

"No, you don't," I said. "What do you want?"

"I told you. I'm collecting for your parents' newspaper subscription." He consulted his pad. "That's $6.80 for this month. But I'll gladly accept your science reports from last year as fair trade."

Jake Picard needed my old science reports about as much as Tom Cruise needs acting lessons. He was the smartest kid in the seventh grade. I wasn't the smartest kid in the eighth grade, but I knew enough not to give him an inch. He'd have me standing there at the door for the rest of my natural life.

"I'll get my dad," I said.

"Does he have old science reports?" Jake said.

While an all-out money search was staged—which produced

$4.79 in change—Jake consumed a half dozen Christmas cookies and told Sara how to solve an algebra problem. I even searched under the couch cushions for money, I wanted him out of there that bad.

"Can you come by tomorrow afternoon?" Mom said. "I'll cash a check and have the money for you then."

"No prob," Jake said. "I won't even tack on a late charge."

I held the front door open for him while he ducked back to the coffee table and scooped up the last cookie. He stopped halfway out. "You going to that Christmas party at Roxanne Pfeiffer's?" he said to me.

I glared at him. "I don't even *know* Roxanne Pfeiffer," I said.

"Yes, you do. She's in our—"

"No, I'm not going."

"Don't beat around the bush, Mj," he said, smiling that obnoxious larger-than-life smile as he breezed out the door. "Just come right out and say what you think."

"Mj, is that the Christmas spirit?" my mother asked.

I just shrugged.

TUESDAY, DECEMBER 18, 8:00 A.M.
ABOARD BUS #318-A

I haven't always been like this about Christmas, I thought as I looked out the bus window. I used to be as squirrelly as Jeremy when it came to dragging out the Christmas albums the day after Thanksgiving. But what was there to be excited about, even at Christmas, when you had this slowly-creeping-up feeling that you're destined to be a nobody?

Everybody had told me junior high was going to be a blast, and I'd spent all of seventh grade waiting for it to happen. I glanced around the bus. It seemed to have happened for everybody but me.

Chelsey Bennett in the front seat had made eighth-grade cheerleader. I had zits and no hips. I hadn't even tried out.

Mike Bach in the backseat was already student council sergeant-at-arms. I hadn't run for office. For Pete's sake, nobody knew me. At the end of seventh grade, exactly twelve people had signed my yearbook.

Across the aisle, Bonnie Sullivan was writing a note—to Blair Anthony, for sure. A lot of girls were getting into the boy thing. I was so nervous talking to boys my tongue turned into a Popsicle.

My eye caught on Jake, up front flapping his lips to the bus driver. Even he had it all over me in one respect. The little dweeb made straight A's. I had to do twice as much homework as I had in elementary school, and I was doing "nice, average work."

I'd always been taught that God had a purpose for each of us. Mine was obviously to take up space.

I looked back out the window, in time to see some men setting up for the live crèche at the Center Street Church. I used to get so excited about seeing the live animals and watching people from the community act out the nativity scene every night for the week before Christmas. This year I couldn't have cared any less if I'd been in a coma.

TUESDAY, DECEMBER 18, 1:30 P.M. JUNIOR HIGH AUDITORIUM

"All right, I want Christmas Past over here, Christmas Present here, Christmas Future right here and—" Mrs. Arnell looked over her glasses vaguely at the group I was standing in. "Crowd, just sort of scatter in this area, and do some business."

The girl next to me stopped popping the rubber bands on her braces and headed excitedly for the nondescript "area" like it was Academy Award material. I followed, tail dragging, and stood with the rest of the "Crowd." Our chorus/drama presentation of Dickens's *A Christmas Carol* was the biggie of the semester, and I should've been nursing a major case of goose bumps over it. But it was tough to get the giggles over being in the Crowd, and it was a cinch a girl like me was never going to be anything more.

"Ps–s–s–t!"

I turned to meet a pair of mammoth glasses perched right at my shoulder.

"What do you want?" I whispered to Jake.

"That's Roxanne Pfeiffer," he said, and jerked his head to my right. I looked at the girl with the braces who was doing Crowd business like a Hollywood extra.

"So?" I said.

"She's the one having the party. You said you didn't know her."

"I still don't," I said. But I looked at her again. No wonder I'd never noticed her. She was just another girl like me.

TUESDAY, DECEMBER 18, 4:30 P.M.
IN OUR KITCHEN

"Half a cup of brown sugar," I muttered. It was like a rock. I banged the box on the counter.

If the shut-ins knew I was gritting my teeth the whole time I was making their oatmeal cookies, they probably would feed them to their dogs or something.

"Bah, humbug!" I said out loud.

The doorbell rang, and I dropped the box on the counter. Saved.

Jake smiled at me over his notepad, the corners of his mouth dipping practically into his eardrums.

"Did your mom cash a check?" he asked.

"Yeah," I answered. "Wait here."

He didn't, of course. He followed me into the kitchen and

plowed his finger through my cookie dough, while I counted out the money.

"Gross," I said. "People are going to eat that."

"What? I'm not people?"

I shoved the money at him. "Here. Think you can find your way to the front door?"

"Just in case he can't, why don't I show him?"

My dad put his hand across my shoulder and patted Jake's. "Women these days, Jake," he said. "No manners, huh?"

They chatted like old cronies on the way to the front door. I picked up the wooden spoon and madly stirred the cookie dough. If I could just get these done before my dad came back . . .

"Marijane—"

He never called me anything except Mj unless I was in pretty deep.

"As soon as you're finished with those, what say we make this shopping trip into an evening? Burgers. The mall. Maybe a frozen yogurt after?"

I gaped at him. He took that for a yes.

TUESDAY, DECEMBER 18, 8:00 P.M. ON CENTER STREET

"I think your mother will like the slippers you picked out," Dad said. He turned the car onto Center Street, and I plopped my yogurt cup into the litter bag without comment. I wanted to say, "Yeah, she'll think of me every time she wears them to take out the garbage," but I didn't. My dad hadn't lectured me yet about being rude to Jake that afternoon, and I wasn't going to do anything to jostle his memory.

"Mj, can I help you with anything?"

I looked at him sharply.

"You aren't having much fun this Christmas, and I just wondered if there's anything I can do."

"No," I said. "I'm fine."

"You're lying, my love," he said.

But he didn't say any more, and neither did I—even when he pulled up to the Center Street Church and turned off the motor.

"Let's get out," he said.

It was the smell that got to me first, and with it the memories. How many years had I run from the car to the rope that separated the crowd from the crèche so I could sniff big and get the animals up my nostrils—the sheep and sometimes a lamb or two, and the donkey.

And then there were the quiet sounds. The way the sheep chattered to each other. The way the donkey shifted his feet in the hay. The way Mary sighed.

I didn't run to the rope this time. But when Dad and I got there, it was all the same. It was the first thing about Christmas that was, and for a minute I forgot to be thirteen and bummed out.

"It's so real, isn't it?" Dad whispered to me.

I didn't answer, but it was. The shepherds were all huddled together, shifting their shoulders and grinning at the baby like proud uncles. Joseph was leaning over Mary and gazing out over the crowd to make sure none of us was going to make a move on his little family.

And Mary herself. She was small and young, and she was looking down at the baby like she couldn't believe this was happening to her.

It was almost as if she could feel me watching her because as I stared, she looked up and smiled. The metal on her teeth shone in the lights, and I gasped.

It was Roxanne Pfeiffer—the girl with the rubber bands on her

braces. The girl who knocked herself out being good "Crowd."
The girl who was a lot like me.

And that wasn't even the half of it. I followed her gaze to the
shepherds she was smiling at, and there he was, stroking the neck
of a very smelly burro and gazing tenderly on the baby. I
wouldn't have known it was Jake without the "mondo"
glasses—except nobody else had a smile that big.

And nobody else had a lump as big as the one I had in my
throat, I know. And probably nobody else was thinking what I
was thinking: *How Roxanne Pfeiffer was probably just like Mary, who
was plain and average and couldn't believe God had picked her to give
birth to the Savior. How Jake Picard was probably a lot like the young
shepherds, who did the same old thing day after day but knew when
something amazing was happening to them—and were ready for it.*

How I was a lot like them and didn't even realize how good
that could be.

I put my cheek against the tweed of my dad's jacket. With a
big sigh, he slipped his hand into mine.

WEDNESDAY, DECEMBER 19, 1:30 P.M. JUNIOR HIGH AUDITORIUM

"Crowd," Mrs. Arnell said, "you're standing there like you're
waiting in line at the express lane at the grocery store."

"Next!" Jake called out.

"Ebenezer Scrooge has just emerged from his house screaming
'Merry Christmas!' You're amazed. Let's show some spirit!"

There was a general groan from the Crowd.

"I want you to watch, uh—"

She pointed to Roxanne, who said her name so softly I'm sure
only I heard it but gave a grin that lit up the room.

"Roxanne and—" And then she pointed toward me. I looked
over my shoulder.

"Mj," Jake said for me.

"Watch Roxanne and Mj," Mrs. Arnell said. "They're over here giving it everything they've got. I believe that they're *excited* townspeople on Christmas morning. I want the rest of you to be like them."

Mrs. Arnell strode back across the stage, and Roxanne and I grinned at each other.

"Did you forget your name?" Jake asked.

"Who made you my interpreter?" I quizzed. But I dug into my pocket and pulled out a bulging Baggie. "Want some cookies?"

He stared at me.

"You had your fingers in the dough. You might as well eat your own germs," I instructed.

But as he took it from me, still stricken, I grinned.

"Merry Christmas," I said.

"You're so strange," he replied.

I shrugged. "What do you expect—from a girl like me?"

Annie Hamilton Donnell

THE
BELOVED HOUSE

Hannah was old. So was Eli. They were too old to do crazy things like running off on their own. But Eli had always had a hard time refusing Hannah's heart's desire, so he gave in.

Hannah wanted to go home. If what they had dreamed for years ever were to happen, it would happen there!

Precious few Christmas stories capture the triumph and tragedy of old age—this one does. Only a mother battered by the onslaught of the years could have written it.

I have long loved Donnell's stories. As moving as are

her "Running Away from Christmas" in *Christmas in my Heart,* book 2, or even her famous classic, "Rebecca's Only Way" in *Christmas in My Heart,* book 3, they fall short of this recently discovered, and long forgotten, story of home. Long may it live on!

The little old face was keen with life. Fires of eternal youth crackled and flamed, not smouldered, in Hannah Bent's eyes. In the glow of them her smallness and fragileness and the ruthless tread of actual years were lost sight of. She fairly glowed up at her old husband from her soft nest of cushions.

"I know what's the matter with me, Eli! I know!" she cried. "And I tell you there isn't another living soul that doesn't know, not even you."

A nervous little hand shot out to smooth his sleeve to atone for the apparent reproof.

"Doctors! I could have told them long ago! Eli, you shut that door tight and stuff the corner of your handkerchief in the keyhole. Yes, yes, or I'll get up and stuff it. I've got something to say that I'm not going to have leak through keyholes. If I don't say it out I'll go crazy—lying here and thinking and thinking it."

Eli Bent, gazing down at the bit of creature, realized the truth of her words and tottered across the beautiful great room to avert the tragedy they suggested. He even stooped to the keyhole.

"There, Heart Dear," he soothed, as he tottered back to her. She caught at his lean old hand in a little frenzy of affection.

"You're good to me, Eli! But you're just as blind as the rest of them. Seems as if you might see—*twenty miles."*

"Heart Dear!" He gazed down at her, startled.

"Yes, that's it—that's the matter with me, Eli. And not another single thing. There never has been anything else. I haven't said a word, but just took all their medicines and their nice kind pitying care till now, this minute. I'm going to take my own medicine now, Eli, and you've got to take a dose, too!"

She laughed jubilantly. The trill of it haunted him; it was the laugh of the maid, Hannah, that he had wooed over half a century ago. The sweet maid, Hannah, looked up at him from the pillows.

"You and me together, Eli!" she exulted softly. "You're not going to desert me this time of day, are you? After fifty-five years of sticking together. No, what we'll do is to take my medicine together as nicely as two 'bent' old pins!" Again the pealing little laugh.

"But-but you kind of scare me, Heart Dear." He trembled, love in his eyes and vague fear in his old soul. His slow wits failed to keep pace with the onrush of her nimble ones. What she had said had a mysterious, awful sound in his ears. She interrupted his thought and abetted it wickedly, with the mischief of a child.

"Eli, Eli, this is a *life-giving* medicine! It means we're going to take a dose together and *live!* It's going to cure us of heartbreakings for home."

Now he understood, and an answering flame to the fires in her eyes kindled slowly in his own. He looked over her head, out of the window—beyond chimney tops—and had his own little vision. The two of them there in the great, luxurious room were looking twenty miles.

"Eli," she whispered, "you see?"

"I see."

"The little path, Eli, and the porch at the front door, and the tangle of bushes beside it that keep *roses* like little birth secrets hid in their hearts? And the oaks we planted to celebrate the babies when they came?"

She was sitting up, gazing with him at his vision.

"And the pump, Eli? The pump!"

"I see it!"

"Well," she exulted, "if the old tin mug's still hanging there, I'm going to have a drink first thing—rust and all. It'll be beautiful, sweet-tasting rust!"

"Heart Dear, lie down—lie down!" tenderly he commanded. He had come back to the great room and her sweet fragileness.

"Not till you promise to!" Hannah Bent returned steadily. It was her ultimatum. "I'll never touch these pillows again till you say, 'Go ahead, Heart Dear. I'm coming, too.' You say that, Eli; say it after me the same as we used to teach the children their little pieces. Go ahead. Say that."

"'Go ahead,'" he faltered, helpless with love and anxiety for his Hannah.

"Heart Dear."

"'Heart Dear.'"

"I'm coming-along-too. Say it!"

"'Coming-along-too.'"

"Why," she laughed, "you say it beautifully! Oh, isn't it a beautiful little 'piece,' Eli? Now I'll reward you. We always give the children rewards. You bring me back that breakfast tray across there, and I'll eat every last crumb on it! Then I'll get up and walk round this room. I'll *run!* The medicine's taking effect already!"

"But-but, Heart Dear," he demurred.

Over the discarded remnants of breakfast she unfolded her bold plans, and they filled him with dismay. He saw obstacles in the way of them too high even for her militant leaping.

"All *you* have to do is to come-along-too!" she interrupted. "I've got every single part planned out. You look here." She drew a paper from under one of the pillows and held it out to him. It was a memorandum.

"Read it—read it, Eli!" And through his spectacles he read the neat little items in a straight little line, as so many, many times in the past he had read her lists when he went down the little path to the gate.

"I'll read them myself—by heart," she laughed.

"'One jar of mincemeat, two pounds of lard, flour, one pound of butter, parsley, and suet and eggs for the stuffing.' I'm going to make some bread and cakes."

Eli Bent's gaze turned slowly to the scintillating, triumphant little old face of his Heart's Dear, and his fears and anxieties vanished; utter faith replaced them. He was ready to follow on behind.

"John and Sue'll find out. They won't let us go, but never mind," he said valiantly. He would hew a way for this frail little wife through an army of Johns and Sues. He straightened up to his full height. It was as if he were feeling the muscle of his staunch old soul and was satisfied.

"John and Sue," softly scoffed Hannah Bent. "Don't you suppose I've got them out of the way? They're going down to Mary Hill's to dinner on Christmas Day, and they're planning to bring ours back to us. I had an awful time bringing them round to consenting to leave us at home. John was determined to carry me down there in a carriage or a *bath chair.*"

Her fine scorn bubbled into gentle laughter.

"When here I am going to take hold of your arm and *run!* Eli, I know just the minute our train home starts."

The yellow folded paper she extracted from another hiding place was, he saw, a timetable.

"There isn't a thing I don't know! We're going to have stuffed fowl and a mince pie. I expect we'll make a good Christmas dinner on that. You're going to stop at James Simmons's on the way up from the station and buy a fowl."

"Yes, so I am," chanted Eli.

"If I'm tired out when I get as far as that—I won't be—you can get James to drive us the rest of the way."

"The house'll be pretty cold," he said. The remark was superficial, scarcely designed to be heard; it was not a remark of soul. As was to be expected, she took no heed of it. If she had answered at all, it would have been to say that the fires of fifty-five warm years lingered in the old house. How could it be cold?

The next day was Christmas Day. With infinite and weary pains, Hannah Bent succeeded in coaxing John and Sue off at a fairly early hour. She was ready for her own start at the bang of the front door behind them. A nervous superfluity of strength possessed her; she had enough for Eli, too. The unquenched youth of her leaped forth at the tune of her key of joy. She sang in a little, thin, sweet pipe as she packed her bag.

"This is salt in this paper. I saved it from my trays of meals. This is pepper, just a little bit for the stuffing; and this paper's got sugar in it. We can get some tea. James's wife'll give us a jug of milk. Now come, Eli. Eli, Eli, we're starting!"

In his care for her he would have carried her home bodily in his eager old arms; but she only clung to his sleeve, hurrying away, fairly dragging him along. A hundred fears assailed her—that they might be late for the train, that the people at the village shop would be away for Christmas Day—or that James Simmons had given up keeping fowls, or even that the beloved little house *might not be there!*

The fears were baseless fears. They got their train, bought their little list of provisions and their fowl, and so came without interruption to the Beloved House. It was there! The two pairs of hungry and thirsting old eyes recognized it by the chimney, by weathered roof and familiar, little, many-paned windows, as the distance slowly lessened.

"Eli, it's the same old chimney. It wouldn't surprise me a bit if the same old smoke came curling out this minute! I'd know the smoke! Eli, do look; there's the broken place in the tiles at the edge of the roof where you went falling over when you would insist on mending it yourself. There's the girls' window and the boys'!" She turned suddenly and lifted a shining face swept clean, by joy, of wrinkles and sad time—havocs—the face of young Maid Hannah.

"Eli, there's our window!"

The small, gray house was set in a fringe of withered snow-covered weeds, but inside it was much as they had left it a year ago. They had taken with them but few belongings to John's and Sue's luxurious home. Even the frail old muslin curtains still hung scantily across the windows of the sacred little parlor. The dust even seemed to have been kind and to have touched but lightly the beloved chairs and tables and soft-tinted old rugs. It was a Beloved Little House of welcome.

They felt no chill. Warm memories lurked in every humble corner and pounced upon them like mischievous children as they made their round of rooms.

"I'm going to take my bonnet off, Eli! It seems almost holy ground we're treading on. We've got *home.*" She was a miraculous, rejuvenated little creature; fragility and weakness seemed no part of her. She went by jubilant soul leaps from blessed spot to blessed spot.

"Here's the old sofa I'd never let you lie on unless you took off your boots. Eli, lie down *with them on!* I'm willing!" She laughed tremulously. "Any minute," she cried, "little John'll come stumping in the house and want a cake. The girls'll be coming downstairs and want to know if dinner isn't ready! Eli, can't you *hear* the children?"

"I hear them!" he assented solemnly. New powers of imagination sprang to life within him to meet her demand. He saw and heard with her. Their rapt old souls took hands and went treading softly over the holy ground.

"I'm well!" the little old wife whispered. "I knew what

medicine I needed. It isn't but a year—just a little year, Eli; but doesn't it seem as if we'd been away twenty?"

"Twenty, Heart Dear," he agreed.

He made her sit down after a while on the old sofa, wrapped deep in his overcoat, while he pottered about the kitchen starting a great fire. He made fires, too, in all the other fireplaces. She appeared before him as he lit the last one and stood—a curiously distorted little figure in the trailing coat—watching the birth of flame.

"It's Christmas Day, Eli!" she said. "There's never been any other just like this one. We never ran away before and got back home!" She bubbled into soft mirth at the new thought that suggested itself. "The children used to run away from us; but we never ran away from the children before! After we've had the mince pie and James Simmons's chicken, and been traipsing together all over the house and the orchard and everywhere else, then we can punish each other for running away! I'll punish you, and you punish me, Eli!" She was gaily frivolous, though in the deep places of her heart were pools of quiet and solemnity.

The December sun was barely warm and made golden blots on the kitchen floor as Hannah Bent got her Christmas dinner. Eli had found his old scythe and was mowing down the crisp dead weeds about the door. She could hear the cheerful swish of it. The kettle sang tender old songs to her from the stove.

It's a freak, she thought, sobered suddenly by a sad little memory that had hovered persistently on the outskirts of her mind and threatened its refound peace. *It's a freak, but I'm going to put on Geoff's plate. I'm going to.* She paused in her work with what Eli called the "Geoff look" stealing over her face; for twenty-five years it had come and gone in her eyes and over her gentle lips, but only for Eli to see.

It'll sort of sadden the dinner; but perhaps Father and I have been feeling a little bit too frisky and happy—perhaps. It was odd how the tender old-time "Father" came with the Geoff look; Eli had always been "Father" in the time when they had Geoff.

I'm going to put his plate on the table; it's kind of borne in on me to do it. If he ever comes back. They had always agreed, she and Father, that Christmas would be the fitting time for Geoff to come. He had been their Christmas child, born to them on the Holy Baby's night. "The Night of Tenderness and Forgiving," had argued Mother softly. "If I were a prodigal son, that's the time I'd choose for going home to my father's house. I'd be certain then of finding welcome." As if he would not be certain any time!

Geoff had been their "odd" child—a curious little creature of whims and fancies, queerly at variance with the calm and stolid little minds of the rest. Where the others plodded satisfiedly in the footsteps of their elders, Geoff had made his own childhood paths and trod them alone. His puzzled little mother had tried to keep step with him but in vain. He had wandered away from her, down a path of fancy too dim and unreal for her passing. When he was but ten years of age she had lost the "feel" of Geoff's little fingers in her guiding hand. At fifteen he had wandered too far, and she lost sight of him altogether. It all came back to her now with pitiless clearness—that first terrified waiting for a son that did not come. He had always come back before—always. Geoff would come. She would wait a little longer than usual—perhaps long after the other children were peacefully asleep—but would hear his whistle down the road at last, and she would go to meet him, as many a time she had gone before. They would walk home together again, she and her odd boy, in their curious fellowship of love that had nothing to do with understanding.

But Geoff had never again whistled down the road. After twenty-five years she was still waiting. Only she, his mother, knew that sometime he would come back; even Eli had failed her in this one particular of indomitable, unyielding faith.

"Here I am, hoping again." She sighed gently. "It's been

coming on ever since I planned us coming home like this. I'm going to put a plate on for Geoff."

Geoff's own plate—she found it and carefully washed away the dust of twenty-five years. It had been the boy's own choice from the scanty stock of picture plates at the village china shop. That day he had worn a little new suit, smart with braid and buttons, that she had made herself. Such a little dressed-up Geoff!

"I'll take the sea plate," he had piped in his small clear voice. "It's got ships on it that sail off and off and off." Later Geoff had sailed off and off and off.

She set the little sea plate on the table and pulled up Geoff's chair. Eli would not mind, because he was Eli. "He'll understand the minute he sees it," she said, her little old face softly alight. "Father'll know it's just me hoping again."

It was curious how easy hoping came today! She caught up the droning tune of the teakettle and hummed a duet with it. It was Christmas—Christmas, the time to have faith in sons. Could a mother stop believing at Christmas, the mother-and-son time of year? She girded her soft old loins in fresh faith and droned on her little humming tune. There were words to it now.

"Christmastime's the time for hoping," sang she.

It was four o'clock when her little dinner was ready. She got down the old dinner horn and blew a gentle blast for Eli. How Geoff, the little tease, had used to pull at her skirt and demand to blow it! Of all the children Geoff had been the hardest to refuse anything. She could hear his little teasing voice now. She turned abruptly back from the door to her pots on the stove. She was no longer young—she was old! Eli was old! The weight of her years and her fragileness slipped back on her shoulders. Yet she set her lips valiantly to smiling curves for Eli when he should come in.

She heard the door open and close behind her, and Eli washing at the sink. The water splashed merrily.

"Eli, what do you suppose I said to myself?" She was trying to gain time to recover her gentle poise of soul. She did not turn round but went on dishing up her dinner. "I said, 'Now likely as not there's one of my old aprons hanging behind the kitchen door.' And *there was!* I've got it on!"

Now she could turn and gaily smile. The washing and splashing were over, and Eli—Hannah Bent uttered a sharp cry, for the face that emerged, pink with rubbing from the towel she had hung on the roller, was Geoff's face. Geoff washing at the kitchen sink!

Father's face looked at her across the crook of the boy's arm; it was full of a wonderment of joy that transfigured its plain blunt lines.

"He's got home, Mother! Here's Geoff! I found him chopping wood for your fire. Geoff always was a master chopper. Mother, Mother, he isn't a ghost! He's *got home!* You always said he'd come at Christmas!"

Neither of them heard his jubilant old chatter. After the instant of utter inability to move or speak, mother and son were in each other's arms. The waiting of a quarter of a century was over.

"Mother," the prodigal boy began; but she would not let him go on.

"Yes, I know—I know! Don't speak it out! You've no need to, dear. Stop just there at 'Mother.' Just say that over and over."

"Mother! Mother!" he said. It was all she needed. The little dinner now cooling was forgotten; it was Mother who remembered it first—-Mother who strove splendidly for a fine matter-of-factness.

"Good gracious," she cried, "if there isn't James Simmons's old fowl getting stone cold! Eli, you and Geoff go in and sit down to your places while I just warm it up a little bit."

In her soul she rejoiced at the plate she had set for Geoff. It had been no freak, but a Providence—she had *expected* Geoff!

The soft hum of Father's blessing stole through the little place of home. At its end, "Wait," said Hannah Bent, and it was as if she said, "Wait, Lord." She bent her small old head over her plate and added her blessing to father's:

"Lord of tenderness and loving-kindness, I thank Thee! As Thou rejoicedest in Thy Christmas Son, I rejoice in mine. Thank Thee, O Lord, for bringing him home."

Margaret E. Sangster Jr.

SPECIAL
DELIVERY!

Feeling sorry for the poor woman, Karen bought the
twenty Christmas cards; then felt foolish, for all her cards
were already sent. Well—not quite all. But the only
way to get them there in time was to Special Delivery
them. In the time in which this story was written,
Special Delivery mail was processed in hours!

It was in the afternoon two days before Christmas that a poor woman, wrapped in a shawl and carrying a basket on her arm, came to the door of the office where Karen Lansing was employed. The woman hesitated on the threshold and Karen, glancing up from her typewriter, saw that an unmasked eagerness lay across the thin face.

"Is there anything I can do for you?" she queried.

The woman stepped hesitantly over the sill. "I've been selling Christmas cards," she told Karen, "and I have just two packages of them left. I thought maybe you, or someone else in this office, might need cards?" Her voice paused on a questioning note.

Karen started to say, *But it's too late, now, to be buying Christmas cards. My cards were bought long ago. They were addressed and in the mail yesterday.* She started to say, *I'm the only one in the office this afternoon—everybody's left for the holiday.* But before she could answer she glanced again into the woman's face, and the excuses died on her lips. She read, in the mute appeal of a pair of tired eyes, what this last-minute sale would mean. It would mean the difference between profit and loss, between success and failure, perhaps between hunger and food.

"How much are they?" she asked instead, and when the woman murmured, "Twenty-five cents a package," she thrust a dollar bill into the reddened ungloved hand.

"You can keep the change," she said kindly. She wanted to add, *You can keep the cards, too, and resell them,* but a proud, aloof quality in that tense, shawl-shrouded face warned her to withhold this last remark.

The woman laid the two packages on Karen's desk. She murmured a phrase, halfway beneath her breath, that sounded like, "God bless you." In less time than it takes to tell, the door closed behind her, and Karen was alone. Alone with two packages of cards that she didn't need any more than a cat needs two tails!

Afternoon became late afternoon. Karen finished her typing

and tidied her desk and began to close the office. She pulled on her modish beret and buttoned her warm cloak and gathered up her handbag. Into the handbag she thrust, in an almost automatic way, the packages of Christmas cards. And then she went home to the room of a boardinghouse where she lived. On the way home she stopped at the florist's to buy a holly wreath to hang in her window and a mistletoe spray to put in a vase on her mantel. She purchased also a supply of special delivery stamps.

It's rank extravagance, she mused, *but now that I've bought the silly cards, I'll use them. I'll send them somewhere, and the special deliveries will guarantee their arrival before Christmas!*

Send them somewhere! Karen, sorting over the cards—and they were very pretty, too—at first could not think of anyone she had neglected. All her friends would receive the messages of greeting that she had sent the day before. A few friends, probably, had already received them! Her relatives—several cousins, and an aunt or two—would receive more substantial remembrances, and so would the two girls who shared her office. Her boss—Karen laughed as she thought of the stern young man who was her employer. Well, she hadn't sent him a card, or a present, either. Probably none of his staff would remember him. And yet, why not? He was a human being, though he was a very repressed specimen, and this was Christmas week. Determinedly she chose the prettiest of the cards, signed her name in the corner of it, and slipped it into an envelope.

"That's one!" she said and went on with the impromptu addressing.

Twenty cards had seemed an insurmountable difficulty at the beginning. But when she got started at them, Karen was surprised to discover that there were ever so many people who would be glad for a cordial message. The florist, for instance, from whom she had bought the holly and the mistletoe; the laundress who did her small weekly wash; the landlady of the boardinghouse; and the lonely old man who sat at a table by himself in the far end of the dining room. Speaking of dining rooms, there was the waitress who served her daily at luncheon in a tea shop in the business district. Luckily Karen knew the girl's name.

Twenty cards, indeed! Six were disposed of, and with no effort! Karen sent the seventh to the cleaner, who had a dingy shop nearby and did her occasional refurbishing. She sent one to the elevator boy in her office building and one to the pastor of the great city church, where she put in a shy, but regular, appearance. She sent a card to the pale girl (obviously an invalid) who lived across the street. She'd seen her often in a window, and she'd made a mental note of the name that was engraved upon the copper door plate. That was ten gone.

The last ten cards weren't quite so easy. But Karen, making a game of it, wrote addresses, with a sparkle in her eyes and a flush on her cheeks. There was that young man—brother of a girl who had worked briefly at the desk next to her own. He had taken her to a concert once and had never called again. Probably, Karen scolded herself, because she'd been too self-conscious to ask him to call. There was the butcher who had refused a coin when she went into his shop to buy liver for a stray cat.

Then, the pastor in the little country church where she had gone as a child. Had he forgotten her? And her first Sunday school teacher, whom she hadn't seen for twelve years. There was the widowed mother of five, who had purchased the old homestead from her father's small estate, and the boardinghouse cook, who never emerged from the basement. She thought of May Kent, a friend from her youth up, with whom she had foolishly quarreled two years before.

I've but one card left, Karen told herself gently. *I'll send it to May. This is Christmas—and Christmas should be a making-up time!*

Twenty cards! They would not have been sent but for a chance impulse of generosity toward an unfortunate woman. Yet, when Christmas morning was still new, Karen began to gather in the fruits of that impulse. For on the breakfast table at her place reposed a wee frosted cake done up in waxed paper, and the boardinghouse manager came over to explain its presence.

"Cook made it for you," she said. "You were the only boarder to send her a card. I loved my card, too. It's folk like you who make a hard profession," she sighed, "easier."

The old man who sat alone came into the dining room while Karen was finishing her breakfast. He walked directly over to her and thrust forth a slender, fragile hand. "I've always thought," he said huskily, "that I'd like to have a daughter who was as pretty as you are, Miss—the name's Lansing, isn't it? I'll mend the thought today. I'd like to have a daughter as sweet and gracious as you are!"

It was in the middle of the morning that Karen, dressing to go out for a stroll in the brisk December wind, heard a knock on her door. She opened it to the small boy from the florist shop, who carried a paper cone in his hand.

"It's a present," he said. "It's from the store." And Karen, pulling off the shrouding paper, saw that the cone contained a corsage of gardenias.

And so it went, all through Christmas Day. The cleaner emerged as Karen passed the shop, which was also his home, to clasp her hand and murmur words in broken English. The pastor of the church hailed her as she went by the imposing brown stone parsonage and came out on his front steps to wish her the joy of the season. The pale girl in the window across the street blew her a kiss from transparent fingers.

Karen returned from her Christmas stroll, feeling that she was part of a dream and that the whole dream was her friend.

And the dream persisted. There was a phone call from the brother of her old friend in the early evening.

"I've wanted, so often, to get in touch with you again," he

told her, "but I thought you didn't like me. I've been walking on air ever since I got your card. Will you let me take you to a party on New Year's Eve?"

Karen's cheeks were shell pink, even though she was talking over the phone, as she murmured her assent.

She went to bed on Christmas night with joy in her heart and a prayer of thankfulness on her lips.

The dream carried over into the next day. The laundress, arriving with a neat bundle, was voluble.

"I never before had had a special delivery letter," she told Karen. "I was that pleased I tinted two of your slips that was faded."

Karen thanked her warmly and went to breakfast. On the hall table she found three letters—one from the old pastor, one from her Sunday school teacher, and one from the mother of five.

"My good wishes have followed you across the years," wrote the pastor.

"I was feeling old and lonely," the Sunday school teacher's feathery writing said, "and you renewed my faith in things and brought a glimmering of youth to my holiday."

The widowed mother of five wrote merely a line or two: "We have been happy in the home that used to belong to your people. I felt sure you'd be glad to know."

Karen, walking to her office, passed the butcher shop. The butcher was opening his door to an early customer, but he shouted, "Any time you want liver for a cat, you know where to come!"

And, as she went by the tea shop, where she lunched, the waitress, just unlatching shutters, slipped out to say, "You're a darlin', Miss!"

Karen laughed and squeezed her hand.

When the elevator boy said simply, "That special message meant a lot, Miss Karen!" her eyes were damp.

But when her boss met her at the door and shook hands soberly and blurted out, "You're a peach, Miss Lansing, to remember me!" the dampness evaporated and her eyes were all asmile. It was seeing the smile that made her boss smile suddenly in answer. And Karen knew, with a sense of complete surety, that her work would be pleasanter from now on and that the wall of ice between the young man and his staff was destined to melt away.

"But why shouldn't I remember you?" she queried.

The boss swallowed hard. He looked at Karen as if he were seeing her for the first time. "Oh yes, there's been a Miss May Kent calling you. She's going to call again, later. She said to tell you she'd received your message and knew what it meant, and she could scarcely wait to hear the sound of your voice!"

Margaret E. Sangster Jr.
1894–1981

Author of "The Littlest Orphan" (*Christmas in My Heart,* book 1), "Lonely Tree" (*Christmas in My Heart,* book 3), "With a Star on Top" (*Christmas in My Heart,* book 5), and "Small Things" (*Christmas in My Heart,* book 6), Sangster was one of the most beloved inspirational writers in America early in the twentieth century. Now a new generation of readers is gathering her to the heart.

HOMEMADE
MIRACLE

Snow is anything but unusual at our Grey House in the Colorado Rockies. But . . . in June? It was snowing the June morning I opened a packet sent us by one of those cherished story collectors who are so crucial to the continuation of our story ministry. After first building a fire in our moss-rock fireplace, I settled down to read the handwritten story.

It quickly gripped me. The large cast of characters and their many subplots worried me because it is incredibly difficult to make such a short story work. As I neared the end, and all the pieces fell into place, I breathed a giant sigh of relief. It being one of those rare stories in which you continually reel back and forth between laughter and tears, I was a basket case at the finish.

There was absolutely no question: It *had* to be included in this collection!

The little town of Chester lay under a light crystalline fall of snow. Every house wore a ruff of icicles, and all the dark blue spruces were bearded with the damp ermine of the season. Through the lamp-lit windows you could see Christmas trees being set up in cheerful living rooms. In the high school auditorium the Choral Club was practicing carols. Above the piercing steeple of old St. John's Church brooded the blue-white radiance of the Christmas star. It was three nights before Christmas, and if you could have written "Peace on Earth, Good Will to Men" at the bottom of Chester, you would have had a first-rate Christmas card.

But you couldn't write it. Nobody knew that better than the Reverend Dr. Ernest Jellicoe, clergyman of Chester, who was at that moment sitting on the floor in the cold, unlighted church, massaging his shinbone. For the fourth time Dr. Jellicoe had caught his toe in the worn carpet in front of the pulpit and fallen sprawling.

The prerequisites of his calling denied Dr. Jellicoe the relief of giving verbal vent to his feelings; but he was certainly in the mood. He was a short-legged, jolly little man, with a rusty thatch of hair, bright blue eyes, and a disposition of belligerent cheerfulness. But now, with the bickering, backbiting, and quarrelsomeness of the Committee on the Community Christmas Tree still ringing in his ears, it seemed to him that St. John's Church was literally falling to pieces.

He stopped deprecating the obtuse pettiness of Mrs. Brittain, Mrs. McManus, Mr. Philbert, and Mr. Dellinger long enough to wonder why some of his wealthy parishioners didn't give the church a new carpet. Miss Leonora Webb, for instance. Her great-great-grandfather had founded the church, and Dr. Jellicoe peevishly groused that Miss Leonora spent enough on that ill-tempered Persian cat of hers to keep this humble temple in unaccustomed luxury. As he mused thus, he sighed. Miss Leonora hadn't been inside the church for five years. In fact, she had vowed never to set foot in it again.

A sense of his own failure swept over Dr. Jellicoe, and in a rush of remorseful feeling he clambered to his knees and prayed for guidance in knitting together the unhappy factions and sub-factions in his parish. He prayed for a new birth of goodwill, the wiping out of misunderstandings and misery, the revival of love and goodness.

"But it would take a miracle," Dr. Jellicoe declared in an after-thought which he did not address directly to the ears of the Almighty. "It would take a miracle."

As he got up and felt his way out of the dark church, he thought how wonderful it would be if everybody in St. John's were like Miss Smollett, the organist—sweet, tireless Miss Smollett, with her wide innocent gray eyes and her small, patient hands. As he turned in at the manse, Dr. Jellicoe felt forlorn and lonely. Christmas had always been hard since Eva died.

Young Mrs. Brittain's problems were somewhat different from Dr. Jellicoe's but just as hard to bear. As soon as the committee meeting had subsided, Mrs. Brittain had sprinted out of the church. She was so tired she could drop, and she had so much yet to do. Mrs. Brittain had been married only a year, and all her husband's family were coming for Christmas dinner.

She now sat at a card table, feverishly wrapping packages, while she reported to Mr. Brittain the goings-on at the meeting. Tom Brittain was lolling comfortably in an armchair, trying to read a newspaper.

"We almost came to blows," young Mrs. Brittain said proudly, "but we won. After all, there have been real candles on the Chester Community Christmas Tree for a hundred years! It's just part of Christmas! It wouldn't be the same with electric lights. It would destroy the whole spirit of the occasion. Don't you think so?"

"Not very safe if you ask me," Mr. Brittain mumbled.

Mrs. Brittain compressed her nice mouth into a thin line. That was the trouble with Tom—always on the practical side.

"Hold your finger on this knot," Mrs. Brittain ordered grimly.

She might have expected Mrs. McManus and Mr. Philbert to be against her. But Tom!

Mr. Brittain threw down his paper with an angry rustle, got up, and lumbered over to the card table. He stuck his finger on the bow, which Mrs. Brittain was holding with such force that one leg of the card table collapsed and the many items on it cascaded to the floor.

"Oh, Tom!" Mrs. Brittain cried. "How could you be so clumsy?"

She could have wept with exasperation at the mess, and Mr. Brittain, now furious, stalked out of the room and pounded up the stairs without a backward look.

Mrs. Brittain got down on the floor and tried to salvage packages, seals, tags, tissue paper, ribbon, and rubber cement. The cement had attached itself to practically every item in the pile and was now seeping merrily into the rug. Everything she touched stuck to her, and Mrs. Brittain finally sat down on the floor and succumbed to tears of weariness and rage. She cried quietly for a few minutes—and then she lifted her head and sniffed, scrambled to her feet, and tore out to the kitchen. Her fruitcake was burning!

Five minutes later she came back with a scrubbing bucket to get at the rubber cement. The light of battle glowed in her tear-stained hazel eyes. The fruitcake was scorched, and it was all Tom's fault.

"He's mean," she muttered. "I don't know why I never noticed it before."

One more quarrel had been added to Chester's oversupply of discord.

"Stand still," Mrs. McManus complained, through a mouthful of pins, to Evelyn, her squirming seven-year-old. "If your costume hikes up in front, you won't look much like an Angel!"

Mrs. McManus was gathering folds of white cheesecloth around Evelyn's tubby middle and sewing loops on the shoulders in order to affix a pair of gilded wings.

"I'm tired," Evelyn whined.

"You're tired," Mrs. McManus said bitterly. *"I* have to finish these two costumes tonight. You know the dress rehearsal for the pageant is tomorrow. There, I guess that will do." She lifted the dress over Evelyn's head. "I can't think," Mrs. McManus said to Mr. McManus, "what Miss Smollett means having that Cermak child in the Angels' Chorus. I honestly don't know what this town is coming to."

"What's the matter with the Cermak child?" Mr. McManus inquired mildly.

"Curtis, you know very well the Cermaks are Polish immigrants. Foreigners!"

"Anna was born right here in Chester," Mr. McManus reminded her. "I remember it well. Her mother died."

Mrs. McManus brushed this off. "I'm sure she hasn't got a pair of white shoes to her name. It'll ruin the looks of the chorus. And she stands right next to Evelyn, too."

"What of it?" Curtis McManus asked sharply. "Joe Cermak is a good man. There's not a better man or a better worker in town. He's done a fine job bringing up that brood of orphan kids. You women make me sick!"

Mrs. McManus stopped speaking to her husband. "Come here, Freddy!" she ordered peremptorily.

Freddy McManus was rolling on the floor with Whiskers, his spotted fox terrier, practically shaking the house with the fervor of their rough-and-tumble.

"Aw, Mother," Freddy complained for the twentieth time. "I don't want to be an Angel. If I hafta wear an old costume, why can't I be Flash Gordon?"

Mrs. McManus looked distraught, even a little terrified. "This is a serious pageant, Freddy," she rebuked him. "I don't want you to make remarks like that."

"Maybe Miss Smollett would let him be Lucifer," Curtis put in. "He seems to be absolutely suited for that role."

"Lucifer! I'm Lucifer," Freddy cried, dancing around in his costume.

Whiskers cocked his ears at this new game and broke into loud barks. In the middle of this bedlam the doorbell rang. Curtis opened the door and was greeted by the sight of the entire Chester police force, a man named Ed Moore.

"Got a complaint from Miss Leonora Webb about that dog," Mr. Moore stated. "Claims your boy set him on her cat."

Freddy picked up Whiskers and clutched him convulsively against his chest. He stared round eyed at the policeman. Mrs. McManus moaned.

"Did you do that, Fred?" his father asked.

"Well . . . uh." Freddy dissembled. "Dad, you know how

Whiskers is about cats. I didn't set him on it—exactly. I mean he just kind of ran after Miss Webb's old cat. In a way."

"Fred, you know what I think about cruelty," Curtis told him. "Go to your room. I'll attend to you later."

Freddy's eyes filled with tears. "Dad," he pleaded, "you won't let him take Whiskers away." His face corrugated with despair at the thought.

"Better keep him penned up," Mr. Moore said kindly. "Just came by to give you a warning. You know how Miss Leonora Webb is—always mixed up in city politics, and we got to pay attention to her. Now me, I don't see a thing wrong with it. Most natural thing in the world. Sets too much store by that old cat anyway."

Dragging up the stairs, Freddy felt relieved; but he looked forward with no anticipation to the impending session, and his hopes for a Christmas bicycle went glimmering.

For years nothing had gone right for Miss Leonora Webb. Sometimes she thought that everything happened to her; but if she analyzed it more closely, she might have come to the conclusion that not enough happened. As a matter of fact, Miss Leonora—now forty-five—was a typical old maid, though nobody in Chester would have dared admit it, least of all Leonora herself.

Miss Leonora was the rock upon which the social wave of Chester split. Up to five years before she had taken a large part in all of Chester's affairs. At that time she had had a falling out with Mrs. Wilford Turner, her best friend, over the decorations of the church for Easter Sunday.

The quarrel had started over some minor issue and had progressed to dimensions possible only in a town the size of Chester. Eventually the two women had stopped speaking, and Miss Leonora had refused to set foot in St. John's Church ever since.

Now every party in Chester was complicated by the fact that Ada Turner and Leonora Webb wouldn't be caught dead in the same room with each other.

Miss Webb lived in the big stone house on the outskirts of Chester with her niece, Kathleen, age nineteen, and her cat, a rambunctious feline appropriately named Jezebel. Kathleen was a sweet, pretty girl with eyes like damp violets, and she had afforded Miss Leonora much pleasure until lately, when she seemed to have become silent, moody and withdrawn. Sometimes she came down to breakfast looking as if she had been crying. Miss Leonora, who never bothered to understand other people, had no way of supposing that Kathleen was in the throes of love and anguish. Miss Leonora would certainly not have supposed that the cause of the trouble was one Wilford Turner Jr.

Miss Leonora lived in a state of perpetual outrage; but today was the last straw. It wasn't enough that Jezebel had come home draggled and bleeding from a dogfight, obviously set in motion by that execrable McManus boy; but now Kathleen wanted to go to that ridiculous Community Tree at St. John's.

It was impossible for Kathleen to explain to her aunt that she hadn't seen Willie Turner for three weeks, after they, like everybody else, had split on the rock of Miss Leonora, and that she felt fairly certain of at least getting a look at him at St. John's and letting him look at her. The name "Turner" was taboo.

Kathleen was already sorry that she had refused to elope with Wilford on December first, thereby risking the loss of his matrimony and certainly cutting herself off forever from Miss Leonora. *Now it was too late,* Kathleen thought, sobbing inwardly. The Chester grapevine had brought to her attention the rumor that Willie was beauing the Masons' visitor from Chicago, a sleek postdebutante named Marcia Garrison, and Kathleen was sick with misery.

"I declare, Kathleen," Miss Leonora finally snapped, "I don't know what's got into you, moping and sniffling around the house, and now this business of the Christmas tree. I can't think why in the world you want to go."

Kathleen got up from the Victorian armchair and stood there, thoroughly angry at last. She said, "Well, I'm *going*. So there. You can't stop me!" Thereupon she turned and rushed out of the room. Miss Leonora shook her head in pure astonishment, and for a brief distracted instant felt like a lonely, cast-off old woman. "What is the matter with everybody?" Miss Leonora asked herself.

Mr. Dellinger was standing behind the counter of his drugstore, worrying about business, although his business went along fine year after year.

The thing that was worrying him especially right now was the alligator cosmetic kit that was supposed to be the outstanding piece of his holiday line. It was marked twenty-five dollars, and it now seemed to Mr. Dellinger that nobody in Chester was going to pay twenty-five dollars for a Christmas present for anybody.

As he brooded, he noticed a couple come along the almost deserted street. They came abreast of the window, stopped, and looked in. He observed that the girl was tall and sophisticated looking and had on a startling hat made of some kind of fur. Her red mouth curved into a smile, and he saw with a thrill of anticipation that her brown eyes were going over the alligator kit. It was that Chicago girl who was visiting Mrs. Mason—name of Garrison or some such. The man with her was Willie Turner.

Mr. Dellinger didn't know whether he liked that or not. Everybody in town (excepting Mrs. Turner and Miss Leonora Webb) knew that Kathleen Webb and Willie Turner were in love with each other. Mr. Dellinger disliked the idea of some city woman coming to Chester and poaching on the rights of a hometown girl. Especially Kathleen.

As the couple sauntered on, Mr. Dellinger added this item to his worry about business, worrying first about one and then about the other. . . .

About fifteen minutes before midnight, a solitary figure came through the doorway. It was Willie Turner.

"Hello, Mr. Dellinger," Willie greeted. "I wonder if I could see that brown alligator case in the window."

Mr. Dellinger was host to a complicated emotion. It looked as if he were actually going to get rid of that kit; but plagued if he wanted to sell it to Willie Turner to give to that stiff-necked Miss Garrison. Why, it would break his heart.

He ambled over to the window and removed the kit from its nest of red satin and set it on the counter. "It's pretty," Willie said, running his hand over the leather. "It's real alligator, isn't it?"

Mr. Dellinger was staggered by his own reply: "Can't say," he replied, "Not sure of it."

"How much?" Willie asked.

"Twenty-five dollars," Mr. Dellinger said. "Too much, if you ask me."

"I'll take it," Willie decided, and Mr. Dellinger winced.

"No exchanges or refunds," he reminded Willie grimly.

"I'll take it along with me." Willie ignored the interruption and laid two tens and a five on the counter.

Mr. Dellinger wrapped up the case and watched Willie go off with his purchase. He felt like a traitor. He felt worse. There had been a time when he could mold public opinion. Now he had merely tried to keep Willie from buying the kit, and Willie had simply brushed him off. His opinions didn't mean anything in this town anymore. He had outlived his usefulness.

I'm slipping, Mr. Dellinger thought as he locked the front door. *I must be slipping.*

Miss Dora Smollett sat before her mirror and minutely examined the lines in her forehead. She sighed. She was just thirty-six; but already the wrinkles were getting imbedded.

Miss Smollett looked around her chaste bedroom and wondered if her life were going to be like this always: teaching school five days a week, playing the organ on Sunday, and every minute in between getting up programs and entertainments for Chester consumption. Not that she didn't love her work; for Dr. Jellicoe was so appreciative of her efforts. He was a darling, really, and lonely, ever since he lost his wife three years ago.

She thought happily about Dr. Jellicoe for a few minutes—how he always backed her up. Tonight, for instance, when that stuck-up Mrs. McManus didn't want Anna Cermak in the Angels' Chorus, Mr. Jellicoe had been behind her 100 percent, in spite of the fact that Mrs. McManus was a power in the church. Anna Cermak had the best voice in Chester, but Dr. Jellicoe didn't know that. He had just backed her up.

To Miss Smollett, Christmas seemed to consist entirely of carols and pageants—the children acting like imps of Satan and their parents acting not much better! If she had a child . . .

Miss Smollett stopped short. It was a strange thing that Miss Smollett, whose waking hours were full of children—mostly brats, too—still wanted a child more than anything. A home, a husband and a child. A husband like Dr. Jellicoe—so gentle and kind and affectionate.

She thought of a little boy with Dr. Jellicoe's rusty red hair and belligerent blue eyes and sighed. She put her elbows on the windowsill and looked out across the snow to the white spire of St. John's and the low-lying bulk of the manse hard by. There was a subdued yellow light in the back window of the manse.

The little town of Chester lay silent and lightless under the tremendous blue arc of the winter sky. A few snowflakes fluttered to earth and piled a little higher on the loaded arms of the blue spruces. In a hundred quiet houses the mysterious processes of life went on—the deep, rhythmic breathing of the sleepers, a child's arm flung out over the coverlet, a man's head settling into the curve of a woman's arm, tears dampening a pillow, eyes staring into the blank darkness while a mind turned a problem over and over, a lonely cough—dreams.

The day before Christmas Eve, every woman in town, with the exceptions of the bedridden Miss Leonora Webb and her niece Kathleen, was buzzing around St. John's Church. At nine o'clock Joe Cermak and his oldest boy had brought the tall, splendid fir, still glistening with melted snow. It was a beautiful tree, stately and majestic. Now it stood in the center of the platform, reaching high into the nave, drenched in blue light from the Memorial window behind it.

Mrs. Brittain was standing on a stepladder, affixing dozens of red candles to the tree's thick, bushy twigs. But Mrs. Brittain's heart was heavy. Tom had gone off to town without kissing her good-bye for the first time in their married life.

She reached for a high branch right at the front of the tree and was suddenly overcome with an attack of nausea. She thought wildly for a minute that she was falling through space. "Tom, Tom!" she whispered, and then the world righted itself. The branch with its red candle snapped back in place.

All around the tree women were busily hanging decorations—strings of tinfoil icicles, tinsel medallions, and artificial snow. They chatted in high strained voices, ran hither and yon. Dr. Jellicoe was there trying to be of some use, though they all thought privately that he was just in the way and ought to go into his study and think up a good sermon or something.

By three o'clock the tree was decorated. The ladies stood back in little groups admiring it. Then they rushed into their wraps and started home to collect the presents, which would soon be piled waist deep around the platform.

All the adults in Chester who were within the pale exchanged their gifts at the Community Christmas Tree. It was a lot of trouble and gave rise to bitter competition as to who gave the finest presents; but, they had been doing it in Chester for a hundred years. The children, who had their real Christmas along with their stockings the following morning, received a toy or two and plenty of candy and nuts from the hands of Santa Claus himself, in a red velvet suit, black fishing boots, and a spurious silver beard. Most of them knew it was Mr. Philbert, the banker, who fancied himself in the role of Santa and certainly had the figure for it.

With a twinge of loneliness, Miss Leonora watched the home-going hordes from the long casement windows in her library. Upstairs Kathleen was wrapping and rewrapping the fine, pin-seal wallet she had bought for Willie's Christmas present, trying to make up her mind whether or not to put it on the tree for him. He might think she was trying to get him back, and of course she wasn't. Still, what earthly use would she have for a wallet with "Wilford Turner Jr." stamped on it in gold? Might as well give it to him—without a card, Kathleen decided—as a last gesture to romance. Then it occurred to Kathleen that Willie might think Marcia Garrison had given it to him; she winced and unwrapped it once more. Finally she slipped it into her purse, unwrapped.

"Ooooh, I'm so miserable," she moaned and collapsed on the bed in despair.

At four o'clock Miss Smollett opened the door to the church auditorium and breathed the wonderful fragrance of the Christmas fir. Her eyes were bright, and a few fragments of her blonde hair had escaped the sensible hat she wore and lay curled against her red cheeks. Dr. Jellicoe, who had come out of his study at the sound, stood behind the Christmas tree, where she couldn't see him, and drank in the sight of her. His heart yearned toward hers, and then he pulled himself up short. What would everybody think?—the preacher and the organist, and poor Eva not three years in her grave yet!

Miss Smollett took off her hat, laid it on the organ bench, and sat down. Then the deep-throated voice of the organ filled the room. Dr. Jellicoe closed his eyes and listened. He felt peaceful and almost happy for the first time in a long while. Then, because his mind seemed to be running entirely too much along secular lines, he tiptoed back into his study.

At 4:15 the first aggregation of Angels struggled in. They were trailed by their mothers, grandmothers, aunts, and sisters, loaded down with Christmas presents, which they began to arrange around the edge of the platform and at the foot of the tree. Thirty minutes of pandemonium mixed with discipline ensued.

Miss Smollett, struggling with the Angels, was beside herself. She decided to put Evelyn McManus and Anna Cermak out in front. They were a perfect foil for each other—Anna with her long dark hair and melting brown eyes and little Evelyn McManus, blonde and pretty as a Christmas doll.

Mrs. McManus sniffed at this arrangement, in spite of the fact that Evelyn would lead the procession. She looked at Anna Cermak coldly. Anna's costume was badly made, and the scuffed toes of her school shoes protruded like clodhoppers from her white draperies.

Finally the rehearsal ended. While the Angels and Archangels were dressing, their feminine relatives stacked and restacked the loot around the platform. Dr. Jellicoe, peering timorously from the study door, found it impossible not to think about the money changers in the temple. But, he reproached himself, they were really all good at heart.

When everybody had left, Miss Smollett sat down in a pew to enjoy the Christmas tree herself for a minute. She closed her eyes and gave herself up to weariness. Presently she wakened with a start, realizing that a man was standing beside her. It was Willie Turner.

"Oh, I'm sorry I scared you," he apologized. "I just wanted to put this on the tree, but I didn't get it wrapped up." He held the brown alligator case toward her.

"Oh, how beautiful," Miss Smollett said wistfully, thinking it must be wonderful to have somebody care for you twenty-five dollars' worth. "I'd put it on just like that. It's lovely."

Willie was grateful. "I'm glad you like it," he said with pride. "Do you honestly think it will be all right unwrapped?"

Miss Smollett opened the case and made little cooing sounds at the sight of the beautiful pale beige lining and the handsome fittings.

"Do you know," she said, "I'd like to open it like this—just the way it was in Dellinger's window."

She set the case, with its lid back, directly in the center of the mountain of presents, right at the foot of the tree.

"Well, if you say so," Willie said doubtfully. "I guess it's all right. Could I drive you home?"

"That would be awfully nice," Miss Smollett answered and got into her coat.

They had a hard time getting the storm door open. It seemed to freeze together in icy weather.

"I keep thinking I'll have to speak to the committee about this door," Miss Smollett said. "It's been sticking for years. I meant to remind Dr. Jellicoe."

Christmas Eve in Chester was like Christmas Eve in any other town, except that the suppressed excitement seemed to reach even a loftier pitch, due to the many challenges thrown down by the Community Christmas Tree. Somehow, everybody got through the day, and by eight o'clock cars were snorting up to the door of St. John's, bearing the citizens of Chester and their progeny, each in his most splendid attire.

Mothers were too exhausted by preparations to have any hope of enjoying the occasion. Fathers were disgruntled; already anticipating the bad news in the form of bills, which would roll in around January first—along with taxes. Children were so wild with excitement that discipline went by the board, and their elders gave up with long, potent sighs. Young people were strangely distraught, already tasting the faint disappointment of an event where anticipation always exceeded reality, knowing in their bones they weren't going to get the presents they wanted most. Quarrels were intensified, feuds more bitter, factions more pronounced. Overworked people were more overworked. Lonely people were lonelier still.

Mr. Philbert, sweating in his red velvet suit in Dr. Jellicoe's study and trying to get his whiskers firmly attached, expressed a cheer and jollity he was far from feeling. He had prudently bought his wife a government bond for Christmas and then discovered at dinner that she had expected a beaver coat. A man never knows what to buy.

Out in front, Dr. Jellicoe was moving among his flock with apologetic hospitality, stopping to speak to every family. They were a fine-looking group of people, he told himself—genuine, honest faces, full of strong American character. But there was a grim tenseness about them all, as if each mind were far away, engrossed in a knotty tangle of its own. Dr. Jellicoe's gentle heart ached. He wanted to bend down and say to them all: "Don't worry. Everything will be all right."

But he wasn't sure it would. Not sure at all.

In a back pew, a little removed, Joe Cermak was sitting with his boys and his older daughter. Joe's big, simple face was lighted with pleasure at the beauty of the Christmas tree, which he had cut down in the woods and for which he felt a special sort of ownership. Besides, wasn't his own Anna in the Angels' Chorus with the rest of the children? If anybody in the room was at peace with the world, it was Joe Cermak.

Then Dr. Jellicoe stopped to speak to young Dr. Redding and his wife. Dr. Redding seemed pathetically glad. He was new in town. He'd come about six months before, to take over old Doc Pierson's practice. But he looked so young that nobody sent for him—a kid like that couldn't know much. Now he and his wife were sitting alone, like two strangers at a feast, nobody saying anything to them.

If I were a real minister, I would know what to do about a thing like that, Dr. Jellicoe castigated himself.

As he was walking sadly down the side aisle on the way back to the platform, he had a sudden impression of drowned violet eyes.

"Kathleen," he cried, "I am glad to see you."

"Oh, thank you, Dr. Jellicoe," Kathleen whispered. "I just had to come."

He peered into her strained, unhappy face. The child was suffering over something. Once again the sense of his futility swamped him. He should have done something about Leonora Webb before now.

Miss Smollett had come out on the rostrum and was walking across to the organ. She wore a soft-blue, velveteen dress. There was a youthful flush on her face. *She looked like a madonna,* Dr. Jellicoe thought—*the Christmas madonna.*

Dr. Jellicoe's heart was like a rock in his breast when he raised his hand and said his simple prayer. He couldn't say the things he wanted to—it would have taken all night. But somewhere far above the little town of Chester his thoughts must have been understood.

When Dr. Jellicoe had finished, the organ's mellow notes sounded and the Angels' Chorus filed solemnly in. The little girl Angels lined up in front of the Archangels. Out in front, on a little promontory of the rostrum, stood Evelyn McManus and Anna Cermak. The polished toes of Anna's little black shoes made the only dissenting note in the company of white innocence. All the Angels' faces were frozen with quiet stage fright.

It all made a beautiful picture; but something was wrong. There was too much strife and weariness in the room, too much struggle and defeat and worry.

Dr. Jellicoe put his hand up to his head. He felt as if his heart would burst. Something had to happen. Something had to relieve this tension. Just as the thin, piping voices of the children began to intone "Silent Night, Holy Night," something *did* happen!

A barbaric noise originating in the basement came screaming up the stairs through a doorway into the church and down the center aisle, accompanied by two hurtling streaks.

Amazement froze the assemblage. Their eyes popped; but nobody moved a muscle, not even the Angels' Chorus. When people remembered it later, it seemed as if the course of events followed the crazy pattern of a comic strip—one of those ridiculous inventions where one object touches another and that in turn sets off another, on down through a long string of idiotic consequences.

Jezebel, the cat, was well out in front; but Whiskers, horizontal with speed, was closing in on her as she tore up the five steps to the platform and took sanctuary in the glistening Christmas tree, spitting and snarling. Whiskers, barking wildly, jumped frantically against the base of the tree. This set the whole tree to quivering, and one candle loosed itself from its moorings and went sailing through the air in a burning curve. It was the candle Mrs. Brittain had affixed just before her attack of faintness.

The immobile audience saw the flaming candle describe an arc and land squarely in the middle of the alligator cosmetic kit, on top of the plastic hair brush. The composition material burst instantaneously into a licking flame, just below the flimsy cheese-cloth dresses of the two smallest Angels.

Panic followed, screams rent the air, and the people began to mill and scramble. Dr. Jellicoe beat at the flames with his bare hands without being able to stifle them. Mr. Philbert burst out of the pastor's study, snatching off his velvet coat as he ran. He threw it over the fire in an effort to smother it; but the flames had spread to the tissue-paper packages and were crackling around the whole platform.

Dazedly, Dr. Jellicoe heard the organ still playing and then the clear, high voice of Miss Smollett directing the children to form in line and march to the Sunday school room. "And I mean it," Miss Smollett cried. "Don't look back!"

The terrified Angels did as they were bidden—all but two. The two smallest Angels stood perfectly still, like terrified ponies, mesmerized by the fire. Curtis McManus, struggling toward the aisle, was forced to stop and lift the inert body of his wife into a pew.

"Move back, Evie, move back," he shouted. "Daddy's coming."

But somebody else was before him. Lunging through the crowd came big Joe Cermak, knocking people right and left with mighty swings of his great arms. A curtain of flames surrounded the platform; but Joe didn't stop. He swept through it, oblivious to burns, swung his powerful body up on the rostrum, and swept the children up in his mammoth clasp. For an instant his big body, a child under each arm, was silhouetted against the background of the giant fir, with fire all around his feet, like some great, prehistoric creature. Then he turned and stalked down the shallow steps, carrying the children like sacks of meal.

With the removal of the most serious peril, Dr. Jellicoe turned his attention to the crowd. Half a dozen women had fainted, and their families were bent over them in frantic efforts of revival. Dr. Redding was moving among them with swiftness and dispatch, giving directions, and they were taking them.

Mr. Dellinger was attempting to bring order out of chaos— standing on the platform steps, shouting orders and giving advice— and people were listening to him gratefully. His twenty-five-year-old knowledge of the aches and pains, the prescriptions and potions, of Chester gentry stood him in good stead.

"Don't raise a window. We can't afford a draft. One of you boys go down to the basement and crawl out through a window and get the fire department."

Even Dr. Redding looked to him for instructions. He was an important man again.

Dr. Jellicoe saw a knot of people about the storm door. They couldn't get it open. He raced down the aisle to the door. He knew its quirks.

"Go to Mr. Mason, Doc," he shouted to Dr. Redding. "He has a heart condition. Might keel over in the excitement. . . . Hey, folks, don't run over Mrs. Willis. This smoke'll be terrible for Grandpa Phelps's asthma! Watch out for him!"

The fire was eating into the carpet now, and Mr. Philbert was running from the lavatory to the auditorium with a scrubbing bucket of water to dump inadequately on the fire. The mountain of Christmas presents was crackling higher and higher in leaping flames.

And a great many odd things were happening. Everybody seemed to take full blame for the conflagration.

"Oh, Curtis," Vera cried weakly. "Whiskers started it all. It's all our fault for not keeping him penned. Oh, what shall we do? To think what might have happened except for Mr. Cermak. Oh, Curtis, I'm so ashamed."

"It was my present that started it," Willie Turner moaned. "That's what I get—that's what I get! If I only hadn't quarreled with Kathy. . . ."

"Jezebel!" Kathleen was weeping. "She must have gotten out when I left. Oh, why did I ever come?"

I told him to put it there, and I'm the one who opened that case, Miss Smollett was thinking in the Sunday school room, where the children were huddled. *If I hadn't been moaning around, I would have had more sense.*

"I knew I never should have bought that fool alligator thing," Mr. Dellinger repeated over and over.

"I might have realized this fire hazard," Dr. Jellicoe said through stiff lips. "I was so busy thinking about myself."

"Oh, Tom, I'm going to faint." Young Mrs. Brittain drooped against her husband's shoulder.

"Patty, what's the matter?" Tom asked anxiously, forgetting they hadn't been on speaking terms for two days.

"But it's all my fault—the fire," moaned Patty. "I *would* have candles, and then yesterday I got to feeling faint up there on the ladder, and I didn't get that one fastened well. That one that fell off! Ooooh."

It was at this moment that Kathleen found Willie in a cloud of smoke.

"Willie," she cried, heedless of his mother, who was being fanned with a hymnbook. "Willie, I'll marry you. I don't care if she turns me out of the house. I love you."

"Kathy!" said Willie. "I was so afraid I'd lost you." He choked on smoke and emotion. "The present I got for you is burned."

"For me?" her voice lifted.

Willie stared. "Of course," he said. "Who else? Marcia Garrison? She's gone back to Chicago."

"Dear God, please let me get this door open," prayed Dr. Jellicoe, "and I'll have it fixed tomorrow. I'll never neglect things again!"

All at once the door *did* open, swinging wide from the other side, and Miss Leonora Webb stood there, glaring.

"Have you seen—," she began, and then caught sight of the pandemonium. "What in the *world!*" exclaimed Miss Leonora and set foot in the church for the first time in five years.

"Miss Leonora," Dr. Jellicoe quavered, "don't go in there. I can't allow you—"

Miss Leonora not only set foot in the church: Wild horses wouldn't have kept her out.

"Is anybody hurt?" she shouted masterfully, as she sailed down the aisle.

A horrible clanging arose, and directly behind Miss Leonora hurtled the Chester Fire Department, wearing red hats and dragging the Chester fire hose.

Miss Leonora was apparently bound for the holocaust to put it out personally; but before she got there, she found Ada Turner, stretched out in a pew in a dead faint.

Miss Leonora didn't stop to reason why. She sat down and began to chafe Ada's hands.

"Put her feet higher than her head, Wilford," she advised the distraught Mr. Turner. "Ada's subject to fainting spells in moments of excitement. Ada, Ada," she said almost tearfully, "pull yourself together. We've got to get out of here."

Miss Leonora was so preoccupied that when she saw Willie Turner kissing Kathleen, it did not even register.

Water was pouring on the leaping flames, soaking the candlelit Christmas tree, to which Jezebel was still clinging, moaning piteously. The flames diminished as rapidly as they had started, and Dr. Jellicoe noticed with sharp relief that in a few minutes they were reduced to smoking embers, with nothing seriously damaged but the Christmas presents. Not a present was intact. From behind the Christmas tree, Santa Claus emerged, soaked to the skin, holding by the scruff of his neck, a cowed and quivering Whiskers. Mr. Philbert had a broad grin on his face. There were always compensations. For one thing, that smoldering mess didn't include a beaver coat for Mrs. Philbert. The firemen put up a ladder and retrieved Jezebel from her lofty perch. When they handed her to Miss Leonora, that worthy took her absentmindedly and said, "I'm so ashamed," and nobody knew whether she was ashamed of Jezebel or of herself.

Joe Cermak had thrown open all the windows to let the cold winter air rush into the smoke-filled church. People began to revive. The atmosphere was pleasanter than it had been all evening—more so than it had been for years. The smoke-blackened, heat-singed faces were happy—happy and grateful and relieved. Families were reunited. Sweethearts were in each other's arms. Friends had come back to the fold of friendship, snobbery had been wiped out and envy and jealousy forgotten, under the stress of common peril.

The great weight in his chest that had been dragging Dr. Jellicoe on for so long dissolved, and he felt free again—free and hopeful. He sensed this change in all his flock, as if the climax had restored to them the use of all their facilities of kindness and understanding. He knew without knowing why that they had made a new beginning in Chester—that it was Christmas in fact.

But something was still missing. Something important. His heart plummeted with terror. Miss Smollett! Where was she? Suppose she had been trampled, burned, overcome with smoke, knocked unconscious by the powerful stream of water? He couldn't remember when the organ had stopped playing. But the organ bench was empty. She was gone!

Dr. Jellicoe raced blindly down the aisle toward the rostrum.

"Dora! Dora!" he cried. He had never called her by her first name before. "Dora!" His voice rose hysterically; but everybody was too busy to pay any attention to the minister.

Except Dora.

Miss Smollett was still in the Sunday school room, trying to comfort the panic-stricken Angels, when she heard her name called. She came through the doorway in her dress of old blue, the light streaming behind her, her hair ruffled into an aura about her head.

Dr. Jellicoe was stricken with her loveliness. "Dora," he breathed, and just as he did so, he caught his toe in the worn carpet and pitched forward once more.

"Ernest," Miss Smollett cried and ran down the steps to him while he scrambled to his feet.

"Dora," Dr. Jellicoe said, "will you marry me?" The light of heaven burned in Dora's eyes.

Mr. Philbert had been going over the church to estimate the amount of damage. He came up and stood beside Dr. Jellicoe and Miss Smollett. "It's a miracle," he said, "how little damage was done. The church is not hurt at all except for the rostrum boards and the carpet. We'll have to have a new carpet."

Ada Turner and Miss Leonora Webb were walking out of the church arm in arm, as if five years of quarreling had not intervened in their friendship.

"There's the miracle!" said Mr. Dellinger. "Would you look!"

All over the church Dr. Jellicoe heard the word: "Miracle." He felt his skull begin to prickle. Three nights before, Dr. Jellicoe had sat right here on the worn carpet and said it would take a miracle. But miracles weren't like that, made out of such homely materials as a cat-and-dog fight. That was sacrilegious! Dr. Jellicoe put the idea out of his mind. But it kept coming back. After all, who was he to question the method by which heaven translates its celestial changes to the earth? How did he know what miracles were made of?

People were beginning to leave now. It was pleasant to hear their voices—not worried anymore about trifles—knowing that trifles don't count.

When they were all gone and he had left Dora at her home, he walked back to the manse, fumbling over the crowded pictures in his mind, trying to sort out impressions and make evaluations. All through his veins ran a strange exhilaration. He stood a moment on the steps looking up at the translucent sky. Dr. Jellicoe wouldn't have been the least bit surprised if it had suddenly split asunder and shown him the heavenly hosts singing, "Hosannah."

There had not been so much peace on earth or good will to men in Chester in more than a hundred years.

Von M. Inger

(TRANSLATED BY HILDEGARD CHAN EPP)

A CHRISTMAS
STORY

Not long ago I received this very old Christmas story
from Mrs. Hildegard Epp of Houston, Texas. In a cover-
ing letter she discussed its ancestry: "This story has been
part of our family's tradition every year. My mother is
from Germany, where she was orphaned shortly after
WW II, and one of the few possessions that she managed
to salvage from her childhood is a tattered and incomplete
book of short stories. It was printed in Old German type.
There are four women in our family, and it takes all four
of us to read this story aloud, because inevitably each

reader becomes choked up and the story must be handed to the next one to resume reading."

What a joy it is to see this very old story live on.

———————————————————

Brrr . . . what a storm! Snowflakes were practically tumbling over each other in their eagerness to reach the ground, and the air was so dense with their teeming activity that only dim daylight reached through into coal miner Struve's small cottage.

A little boy was kneeling on a bench, chin in his hands, immobile as he gazed out the window. At first he laughed with enjoyment at the exuberance of the snowflakes, but as it began to snow harder, his expression slowly changed to one of concern.

"Mother, Mother!" he called as she stepped into the room, "it's becoming awfully stormy! The little angels are not going to be able to get through for Christmas!"

His mother stayed for a moment to look out at the winter storm.

"Ei, Andres," she comforted, "that won't trouble the angels. After all, they can fly."

"Of course, they can fly!" He was consoled by the thought. But then another thought made him reach out to take hold of the corner of his mother's apron before she could hurry away.

"Mother, Mother, how terribly much I would like to have a little Christmas tree! Do you think that I may get one? Do you?"

A Christmas tree . . . yes, in past years, their family had done well enough to be able to share gifts with their children in celebration of the Christ child's birth. Since then, however, the father had become so sick that most of their meager savings had been used for the hospital bills, so that lately at times there had not even been a dried loaf of bread to eat in the house. Last year she had been able to decorate their large Geranium tree with candle stubs and foil-paper pictures; that had become their Christmas tree. But even this tree had since died, and now there was nothing left for the children to look forward to, nothing. . . .

"Mother, Mother!" a voice sounded into her thoughts, "I would so much like to have a Christmas tree!"

"Andres," a frail voice spoke from near the cottage stove, where the invalid father sat sunken in a chair near the heat. "Andres, have you not a rich heavenly Lord Jesus? Tell Him your request, maybe He will grant it to you."

Softly pulling her apron out of the little boy's grasp, the mother gently wiped it over her eyes and stepped hastily into the kitchen. Andres, however, slid quickly down from the bench and slipped into the bedroom, where he kneeled down in the corner. How often in the past had he seen his devout father do likewise in this very corner!

A few minutes later a happy clattering of wooden shoes was heard at the cottage door. Four lively children, who had been heartily playing in the snow on their way home from school, tumbled into the front room, and four high voices cried out simultaneously to tell Father how wonderful it was outside. But Mother propelled them all outside at once, because they were not to bring so much cold and dampness into the room where their father was so ill. Only after they had suitably clapped off all the snow and warmed themselves at the stove did they gather hopefully around the cottage table. Soon Mother came out from the kitchen with a pan filled with baked potatoes and placed it in the center of the table. The potatoes, constituting their entire meal, had been carefully divided into five portions, so that no child would come too short. Here, where poverty dwelled, every last morsel was important. But there was no grumbling from the five children; in thanks they had folded their hands for a moment of grace and then gave themselves entirely over to the potatoes as twilight crept quietly into the room.

In a large, beautiful house in the middle of the sprawling village another group of children were also gathered around the table in the family room. A hanging lamp shed a pleasant glow over the room, and in the tiled wood furnace large logs provided a merry warmth. There was no hint in this warm and well-lit room of the turbulent storm outside, except an occasional soft rustle as small drifts of snow slid down the windowpanes. A cozy peacefulness reigned in the room, which the mother, sitting in the midst of her six children, seemed to perceive in her inner spirit as well.

"My goodness! Just look at that snow!" exclaimed Kurt. "That will be great for sledding on Christmas Day!"

"But it will spoil the pond's surface," responded his oldest sister wistfully. "Just now the ice is as smooth as a mirror."

"And I just wished for ice skates for Christmas, too," the second sister almost pouted as she glanced reproachfully out the window.

"Oh, so therefore it should stop snowing just for you?" teased her brother. "You girls just don't know how to enjoy a good snow, and anyhow, Hans Peter says that snow is good for the grain. Isn't that so, Mother?"

Even without his mother's confirmation, Kurt would not have doubted Hans Peter's assertions, because Hans Peter was the farm's foreman and the resident Master of All Trades in the house.

At this point the mother suggested they all sing a Christmas carol. "Yes, yes!" they cried, "that will put us into the Christmas spirit!" So they sang, and even Trudchen, the youngest, squawked out here and there, whether it fit or not, "O kissmass tee, O kissmass tee!"

That the children were engaged in Christmas preparations was apparent by the large pile of colorful paper and sugared treats that were piled in the middle of the table. They were making decorations for the Christmas trees that they were planning to give to the poorer families in the village. Following Mother's directions, little baskets, cornucopias, stars, and little banners were being constructed out of the colored papers. Even Trudchen worked with them in her own way. Her chubby little fingers bustled eagerly among the colorful snippets, and she imagined herself to be very helpful. She spread out before her a few of the paper snippets, which she fancied to have the shape of hearts.

"Oh, oh—wots of widdle hearts!" she cried happily. "Tudi want to give dese to all de widdle angels."

"And just how are you going to accomplish that?" asked Kurt with a good-natured laugh at her side.

"Tudi sends them wit de wind."

"But they will all fall back down, because the earth pulls all objects toward itself. Isn't that so, Mother? And Hans Peter says . . ."

"Oh, oh!" interrupted Trudchen with a wail. "Den widdle Baby Jesus won't get any?"

Despondently she looked at her small supply, which in her thoughts she had already given away as gifts. But then the nanny appeared, leaving Trudchen no more time to reflect. Trudchen knew it was no use escaping when bedtime came around. Resolutely, therefore, she swept her small treasures into her apron. "Tudi still has a heart weft, in here," she said, pointing to her chest. "Widdle Baby Jesus gets dat one—but just one piece," she corrected herself as the nanny held her up to her mother for a goodnight kiss. "De other piece is for Mama!" and the chubby arms clung tenderly around her mother's neck.

"Mama," said the oldest daughter, when Trudchen had been borne away. "Struves also have a sweet little boy, almost as sweet as Trudchen. Couldn't we also give them a Christmas tree?"

"Hans Peter says that Struve family is awfully poor," remembered Kurt.

"Is that so?" The mother rested her hands for a moment and looked thoughtfully at them. "How sorry I am that you didn't mention this sooner, but now I have only ordered six little trees, and it is too late to order more."

Poor little Andres, for how can there be a Christmas tree for you now? For there is otherwise no one who will have ordered one for you, and in these treeless plains there were no forests where a tree could have still been fetched. Poor little Andres!

"The Christmas trees have arrived!" Kurt shouted the news into the living room the next day, and everyone hurried onto the porch. Even Trudchen waddled out. But as she noticed the delivery man, wearing a worn stocking cap with icicles clinging to his beard and looking every bit the description of Knecht Ruprecht, she turned back in haste and peeped out from behind the door.

Everyone stood around admiring the fir trees. Here was their own tree—how full and tall it was!—and here were the trees for the needy families! One-two-three-four-five-six . . . *what?* The children stared in wonder upon a seventh little tree shyly leaning against the others.

"It must have been an oversight," concluded Mother, "because I know I had ordered only six trees. But the tree is here now, and now the Struve family will be able to have one after all!"

Christmas Eve! The church bells rang in the Holy Night and proclaimed in exulting chimes the age-old tidings of good news: Joy to the World, the Lord has come! A festive and expectant mood spread out across the village, and in each of the homes people everywhere were approaching the Christmas celebrations in their own particular ways. Some found the highlight of Christmas in the elaborate holiday meals. But oh! how soon their enjoyment came to an end. Others viewed the sharing of presents as the core of Christmas, and without gifts there would have been no Christmas for them. Poor, needy people! But whoever looked up with gladness and hope to the Son of God, who became Man for our sake and who exchanged Love for love, these were the people who celebrated a joyous Christmas, whatever their outward circumstances may have been.

To the latter surely belonged the miner Struve, who despite illness and poverty had just given thanks with his family to the Lord for His love. Now he sat sunken down near the stove humming a Christmas carol, while in the kitchen the children were watching how Mother was preparing their simple meal.

Suddenly the cottage door jingled quietly, and from the next room were heard stifled footsteps and whispers. The children looked up at each other in amazement. Only Andres, who quietly folded his hands together, did not wonder—because he *knew!* Hadn't he earnestly brought his request to the Lord Jesus day after day, and now He was here, now He had surely come with the dearly wished for little Christmas tree!

"Stay here!" commanded Mother quickly, "I will go and see what is happening." And she slipped into the living room. Soon she returned, tears in her eyes, and beckoned the children into the room. Oh, wonder! There in the middle of the room stood a shining Christmas tree, hung with beautiful decorations, and it was accompanied by children's voices singing, "O come, all ye faithful. . . ."

Andres was a bit surprised that he didn't actually see gleaming angels in the room but merely human children of flesh and blood, who in addition seemed to have familiar faces! But the mother of these children, who had just heard the story of Andres's daily prayers from the Struves, now knew why the seventh little tree had been delivered to her house. The hand that, without human oversight, had felled the extra tree, had been guided by the hand of the Lord, for whom even the stammering of a small believing child becomes a mighty force in heaven. The mother bent down therefore to little Andres and whispered into his ear, "This little tree was sent to you by the Christ child. . . . He asked us to bring it to you."

Stefan Zweig
(TRANSLATED BY EDEN AND CEDAR PAUL)

THE LORD
GAVE THE WORD

George Frideric Handel was broke. Creditors besieged him night and day. So great was his stress that he was felled by a stroke. Doctors shook their heads: "He will never write again!"

But the Lord was not through with His servant. There was a reason why he was restored to life and strength. That reason came to Handel one evening when he was convinced that his life, career, and happiness were over.

Then the Lord gave the word.

George Frideric Handel's manservant was strangely employed on the afternoon of April 13, 1737, as he sat at the open window on the ground floor of No. 25 Brook Street. To his annoyance he had found that he was out of tobacco.

True, he needed but step over to Mistress Dolly's, a few streets away, in order to replenish his store. Yet, because of his master's irascibility, he dared not venture from the house at this particular hour. The choleric German had come home in a terrible fury from rehearsal, red in the face, his temporal arteries distended and throbbing visibly. He had banged the front door behind him and was now stumping up and down the room overhead, walking so furiously and heavily that the ceiling shook alarmingly.

On such days it was not wise to be lax in duty.

Still, the man felt he must do something to relieve the tedium, and so, instead of puffing blue smoke out of his short clay pipe, he amused himself by blowing soap bubbles from the casement. Having prepared a nice little bowl of soapsuds, he launched the bubbles into the street. Passersby stopped to stare at the show, some chasing the pretty balls with walking sticks, all laughing and enjoying themselves vastly, but none of them showing the least surprise. For they were used to hearing and seeing strange happenings around this house: a great outburst of music from a harpsichord or shrieks and wails from the throat of a lady singer on days when the maestro was in one of his berserker rages because the artist had sung a trifle sharp or a little flat. The neighbors, living in Grosvenor Square, looked upon 25 Brook Street as a lunatic asylum.

The manservant cheerfully continued blowing his iridescent bubbles, becoming more and more deft at their production, launching them with ever increased skill into the air, until at last one actually floated over to the first story of a dwelling across the street. Suddenly his game ceased, and he sprang to his feet. A heavy thud, followed by the sound of broken glass, had come from the room upstairs. In a trice the man was on the landing above and entered his master's study.

The chair Handel habitually used when at work was empty. Indeed, the room itself appeared to be unoccupied, and the servant was about to make for the bedchamber when he caught sight of a body lying motionless on the floor, its eyes fixed and open, while from its mouth came a dull, stertorous rattle. For a moment, fear kept the fellow rooted to the spot. Groans issuing from the palsied lips came jerkily and grew weaker and weaker in tone.

Christopher Smith, the composer's amanuensis who was at work in the story above, likewise heard the commotion and hastened to the scene of the disaster. The two men raised their heavy burden from the floor, and as they did so the arms dangled loosely from the shoulders. Having made their master as comfortable as possible and propped up the lolling head, Smith turned to the servant, saying, "Better undress him, while I run for a doctor. Sprinkle his face with water, until he comes to."

Not stopping for an instant, Christopher Smith hurried along Brook Street and made his way toward Bond Street, hailing every hackney carriage that passed at a slow trot. But none of the drivers took the slightest notice of the podgy, breathless man racing along in desperate haste. At last Lord Chandos's coach came rolling by. The occupant recognized Smith, who, forgetting every law of etiquette, wrenched open the carriage door.

"Handel is dying," he cried unceremoniously to the duke, who was a music lover and the most generous patron of his beloved master. "I must fetch a doctor."

"Jump in," said His Grace, shouting an order to the coachman.

The horses were whipped up, and Dr. Jenkins was dragged from his rooms in Fleet Street. He and Smith leaped into the doctor's gig and drove swiftly back to Brook Street. On the way, Handel's familiar explained: "They've worried him to death. He was so vexed, so furious with those . . . singers, and those quill-driving criticasters, and what not. Think of it! No fewer than four operas has he composed this past twelvemonth, hoping thereby to save the theater from perdition. But it's no good; everyone's against him, especially the Italians, headed by Senusino, who is nothing better than a bellowing monkey.

"Ah, you cannot know what they've made our Handel suffer. All his savings have been swallowed up in these ventures: ten thousand pounds! And now his creditors are dunning him to death. Never before has a man worked more gloriously, been more forgetful of self. But they are determined to break our giant. Ah, what a man! Ah, what a genius!"

Dr. Jenkins, cool and collected, listened to the diatribe. Before pulling up at No. 25, he inquired, "How old is he?"

"Fifty-two," answered Smith.

"A ticklish age. He's worked like an ox—but then, he's as strong as an ox. Well, it remains to be seen what can be done."

———

As the manservant held a basin and Christopher Smith lifted Handel's arm, the doctor made an incision for the necessary bloodletting. As soon as the blood spurted forth, a sigh of relief came from the flaccid mouth. Handel drew a deep breath and opened his eyes. Their expression was unconscious, weary, faraway; their light was extinguished, and they looked glazed.

Dr. Jenkins bandaged the arm. Nothing much could be done for the moment. As he was about to get to his feet, he noticed that his patient's lips were beginning to move. He leaned forward to catch the halting words:

"I'm finished—no strength. Don't want to live . . . without strength."

Bending lower to get a closer view, Dr. Jenkins perceived that while one eye stared sightless into the void, the other was conscious of its surroundings. As a test, he raised the right arm of the stricken man. When he let it go, it dropped lifeless. Then he tried the left. This remained in the position wherein he placed it. Dr. Jenkins was no longer at a loss for a diagnosis.

Smith followed him from the room and asked anxiously, "What's the matter with him?"

"Apoplexy. Right side paralyzed."

"And is he . . ." Smith hesitated a moment; then said, "Is he likely to recover?"

Dr. Jenkins took a pinch of snuff. He did not like being catechized in this forthright way. "Maybe," he answered dubiously. "Anything is possible."

"Please, please tell me if he will be able to work again."

Dr. Jenkins was already descending the stairs. He halted and murmured softly, "I'm afraid not. We may save the *man,* but the musician is lost for ever. It seems to me that his brain has been permanently injured."

Smith stared before him nonplused. Such a look of despair came into his eyes that the physician was touched.

"As I said before," he added consolingly, "one never can tell. A miracle may happen. True, I've never seen such a one; but—"

During four long months the right side of Handel's body remained as if dead. He could neither walk, nor write, nor force his right hand to sound one of the keys of the harpsichord. He could utter no word; his lips were flaccid; a few syllables came lolling from his mouth.

When friends made music for him, his glance would light up, and his poor heavy frame, as in a dream, tried to sway rhythmically to the measure, but his limbs were as petrified as if they had been frozen, and horror invaded his eyes. The muscles no longer obeyed the nerves, and the giant felt himself walled up in an invisible tomb. When the music ceased, his lids closed, and his face took on once more the aspect of a corpse.

As a final and desperate remedy, the doctor ordered him to Aix-la-Chapelle for hot baths.

Now, just as under the frigid earth there boiled and bubbled the strange hot springs of Aix, so within the petrified body of the great musician there stirred a mysterious force: Handel's will, the primitive urge of his being. This had not been touched by the stroke, and the undying fire refused to be quenched under the load of the finite body. The giant had never yet been conquered; he wanted to live; he desired to create; and so mighty was this desire that it brought about a miracle that ran counter to all the laws of nature.

The specialists at Aix warned him against staying longer than three hours in the hot baths, saying that his heart could not stand the strain. But to their dismay, Handel remained nine hours at a stretch in the water, and his determination, his will, brought him strength. A week after his advent in Aix, he was able to walk; another week, and he could raise his arm. What a triumph of Will over Caution! Handel dragged himself from the palsy of death and grasped at life with enhanced ardor, with the glowing enthusiasm of a sick man who knows that health is to be his once more.

On the day he was to leave Aix, now again master of his life, Handel halted before the cathedral. He had never been fervently religious. Yet, with the new surge of vitality within him, he felt moved by an irresistible force. There stood the huge organ. Slowly Handel set himself to improvise, and gradually the fire of inspiration invaded his being. Glorious chords rose and fell, filling nave and aisles with a clarity of sound, which the nuns and other pious persons at their devotions below had never heard on earth before.

Handel, his head bowed in humility, played and played. He

had again found his method of expression, the language in which he conversed with God, with his fellow mortals, and with eternity. Once again he could compose music. At last he felt that in very truth he was cured.

"I have come back from Hades," declared Handel proudly as he threw out a mighty chest and stretched his no less mighty arms.

He said this to his English physician, who marveled at the medical wonder produced in his patient. Henceforward with erstwhile fury and energy, Handel hurled himself into the work of composition. He was now fifty-three, but there was no diminution in his enthusiasm for inspired labor. He wrote an opera— how willingly his hand obeyed his behest! There followed a second, a third, a fourth; then the great *Saul, Israel in Egypt,* and *Alexander's Feast.* It was as if a boring had been made, and a spring, long pent up, were tapped. Inexhaustible waters flowed forth freely.

Nevertheless, fate was against him. His pension stopped; then came the Spanish wars. Crowds assembled in the public squares and market places, but the playhouses were empty. Debts mounted. A merciless winter followed. So cold was it in London that the Thames froze, and skaters swarmed on its surface. Houses of entertainment were closed, for there was no means of heating them. Singers went hoarse, engagements were canceled, Handel's situation became desperate. Creditors pressed him from every side; music critics sneered; the public remained cold and indifferent.

Handel gave a benefit performance, which saved him for the moment, but in 1740 he felt that he was a conquered and smitten man. The mighty stream of inspiration seeped away into the sands; his refreshed and reinvigorated body wilted likewise.

Why did God permit my resurrection, he asked himself, *only to allow my fellowmen to bury me again?* And in his wrath he murmured the words of the Crucified: "'My God, my God, why hast Thou forsaken Me?'"

A lost soul, a man whose heart was filled with despair, who was weary of himself, who no longer believed in his own energy of creation, whose faith in God had, perhaps, lapsed—such was Handel during those dreary months in which he wandered about the streets of London. He did not dare to return home until far into the night, for he knew that many creditors would be waiting on his doorstep. As he rambled along, he felt that passersby glanced at him indifferently or scornfully. At times he stood motionless before a church, thinking to enter the fane; but he knew too well that words would bring no comfort to his tortured soul. Another day his feet led him to a tavern; yet a man who has experienced the intoxication of spiritual creation can find no inspiration amid the fumes of alcoholic liquors. The bridges crossing the Thames allured him, and as he gazed into the dark and sluggish waters, he wondered whether one plunge into their muddy depths would not be the most suitable exit.

The burden of loneliness, the feeling that he was forsaken by God and man alike, was intolerable.

On August 21, 1741, he returned from one of his interminable walks. The day had been hot as molten metal, with the burning cup of the sky arched over a breathless London. Not until nightfall had Handel issued forth, hoping to find a little freshness amid the trees in Green Park. He was tired, oh so tired, as he flopped to a seat amid the shadows; tired of talking, tired of writing, tired of playing music, tired of thinking, tired of feeling, tired of life itself.

And now he found himself back in his study. Mechanically, as for so many years he had done, he lit the candles at his worktable. In the old days there had invariably been some task to finish. He had always come back from his walks abroad with a melody, a theme, that required elaboration. But this night there was nothing; the mills of fantasy had ceased working; the stream was frozen and still. There was nothing to begin or to finish. Handel was faced by emptiness.

Emptiness? Yet no! What might that white-paper parcel be, set so carefully in the middle of the table? Handel picked up the packet and felt it delicately with his finger tips. Then he broke the seals. A letter, with a bulky manuscript. A letter from Charles Jennens, the librettist. He informed Handel that he was sending a new text and hoped that the "phœnix musicæ," the greatest genius in the realm of music, would deign to accept the lumbering words and speed them forth on the wings of his undying melodies.

Handel dropped the missive as though it were some loathsome reptile. Was Jennens laughing at him? A mean thing to scoff at a dying man, stricken as he was with paralysis! The musician, in his despair, tore the letter to shreds, threw these on the floor, and stamped upon them viciously.

Jennens had turned the blade in Handel's sorest wound; his heart was bitter within him. Fretfully he extinguished the candles and groped his way into the bedroom. Throwing himself onto the bed, he burst into a fit of weeping.

Sleep would not come. A storm was raging within him, he was restless, troubled by an evil and mysterious disquiet. He tossed and turned, now on his right side, now on his left, becoming more and more wakeful as hour followed hour. Should he get up and cast an eye over the text? No! What would be the use? He was no better than a corpse. He had been cut off from the stream of life. God had forsaken him! And yet vestiges of his innate energy spurred him on; a strange curiosity encompassed him, forcing him, in spite of his gloom, to rise, to go back to his worktable, to relight the candles there, though his hands trembled. Was another miracle about to be performed? Was his mind to be relieved of its paralysis as his body had been freed from the inertia following upon that stroke? Perhaps God would deign to give him healing and comfort for the soul.

Handel pushed the sheets of manuscript nearer the light. On the first page he read the words: *The Messiah.* Another oratorio! His earlier achievements in this medium had been failures. With feverish hands he turned the title page and began to read: The first words arrested his attention.

"Comfort ye."

A marvelous beginning; but not merely that. The words were an answer, a divine answer, an angelic summons to his weary heart.

"Comfort ye."

The syllables reechoed in Handel's mind, stimulating him, assuaging his anguish. Hardly had he read them than they began to translate themselves into a musical idiom, swelling, calling, singing forth into the ether. The portals had been thrown wide. Oh, joy! Handel heard musical tones once more after the long dearth of inspiration.

With trembling fingers he turned the pages of the libretto. Every word seemed to seize him with overwhelming power.

"Thus saith the Lord."

Was this not addressed to him personally? The fist that had smitten was now opened; a heavenly hand was raising him from the earth.

"And He shall purify."

Truly such was happening here and now with him, for grief and gloom were scurrying from his heart, and light was penetrating within, crystal-clear and pure. Who else could have put such sublime words into poor old Jennens's head, who else but He who knew the need of an unhappy creature? Certainly the pen of the insignificant poetaster in Gopsall could never have been spontaneously inspired.

"That they may offer unto the Lord."

Yes, kindle the sacrificial flame within an ardent heart, a flame that would leap heavenward. To him alone had come the summons to lift up his voice with strength; aye, to cry out with the full blast of tubas, of mighty choirs, of thundering chords on the organ, so that, as on the first day of creation, the Word might rouse all those who still "walked in darkness."

"The angel of the Lord came upon them."

With shining pinions he had entered this room, had touched the sufferer and brought release. How could mortal lips remain silent after such a visitation, how not rejoice and lift up voice and heart in jubilant song?

"Glory to God!"

Handel bowed his head over the sheets of paper before him. All sense of weariness disappeared. Never before had he been so conscious of the torrent of creative force within him. He was bathed in the warm and soothing rush of words, words which penetrated to his inmost being, bringing him a sense of exultant liberation.

"Rejoice!"

The word rose and drummed on his ears. In spite of himself, he raised his head and spread wide his arms. One who has suffered much is alone capable of rejoicing; it would be Handel's mission to testify before men how suffering had uplifted him.

When Handel came to the phrase "He was despised," the words struck home; memories of recent distress surged up. The world had looked upon him as vanquished, it had already buried his living body, it had scorned him. Nevertheless, "He trusted in God, and God did not leave His soul in hell."

No, God had not left Handel's soul in the hell of hopeless impotence but summoned him forth to action so that he might bring tidings of great joy to his fellow mortals.

"Lift up your heads," he now read. How commanding were the

tones! Then of a sudden Handel felt nonplused, for he read in poor old Jennens's handwriting the sentence "The Lord gave the word."

Handel held his breath. Truth had issued from the pen of an indifferently gifted man. Surely the Lord Himself had inspired this second-rate poet!

"The Lord gave the word—" Divine mercy had rained down from on high. The stream must flow back to the Godhead in songs of praise. The notes must catch up the words and toss them far and wide; the words, which were but mortal, must be converted by sheer beauty and fervor of spirit into imperishable sound. Again and again must the liberating syllables be repeated: "Hallelujah! Hallelujah! Hallelujah!" for all eternity.

The voices of mankind must be brought together in a mighty chorus; high voices and low, the unflinching tones of men mingling with the softer tones of women. Like a Jacob's ladder of sound the notes must rise and fall; sweet notes from fiddles merging into the rougher notes from the brass, the whole sustained by the powerful undertone of the organ.

"Hallelujah! Hallelujah! Hallelujah!"

Yes, thought the master, *out of this single word must rise a song of joy so formidable that it will reach the throne of the Creator.*

Tears flooded Handel's eyes as the fires of inspiration invaded him. There remained a few more pages to look at: the third part of the oratorio. But the composer's strength seemed to have ebbed with that mighty exclamation of "Hallelujah! Hallelujah! Hallelujah!" The melodies those words had inspired swelled and filled his whole being, burning like liquid fire. The phrases pressed upon him so that his frame felt too small to contain them; they wanted to escape and storm the heavens with their melodious roar.

Handel took his pen and jotted down notes; quicker and quicker the queer little signs began to cover the paper. He could hardly contain himself. Like a ship whose sails are filled with a stiff breeze, Handel was carried forward on his musical voyage.

The night was calm and silent around him, darkness and peace lay as a pall over the huge city. But light flooded his own soul, and (though the sounds were unheard by others) the study was alive with the music of the All.

———————————————

When Christopher Smith cautiously entered the room next morning, Handel was still at work. And when he was asked whether there was any copying to be done, Handel's only response was an ominous growl.

Nobody ventured thenceforward to disturb the master for three weeks. When his food was brought, he merely crumbled a piece of bread with his left hand while continuing to scribble with his right. He was as if intoxicated. When he marched up and down the room, beating time with his hand and singing at the top of his voice, his eyes looked distraught; if someone addressed him he started, and his answers were vague and disconnected.

During these days the domestic was hard put to it to keep his temper. Creditors presented themselves, singers came begging the maestro to produce some cantata or other that might show off their particular talents. Handel was invited to give a concert at court. Such people had to be placated and sent away hopeful, for if the man ventured to ask his master, he was confronted with leonine fury and flashing eyes.

Time and space, during these feverish weeks, were obliterated so far as Handel was concerned; day and night he kept hard at his job, living wholly in the realm where rhythm and tone reigned supreme.

At last, in three weeks—an unprecedented marvel in the world of composition—the great work was finished. It was now September 14. Words had been transformed into music; imperishable sound had issued from dry vocables. A miracle of human will had been performed, just as aforetime a dead body had been raised from the dead.

One word alone remained to receive inspiration: the final "Amen." But these two abrupt and short syllables were now built into a monument that was to reach to the skies. One voice tossed it to another; the syllables became long and protracted, to be reknit and then rent apart. The composer could not have enough of the word, dwelling upon the first vowel so that (the organ sustaining the chorus), it could fill, not only a cathedral but the very dome of the sky.

One fancies that the angels have joined in the p'an, and that we hear their voices ringing among the rafters of heaven. Here only is it that the echoes of his everlasting "Amen, Amen, Amen!" die away.

At last Handel rose to his feet. The pen slipped from his hand. He neither saw nor heard anymore. Tired, yes, that was what he felt, infinitely tired. Clinging to the walls, he stumbled toward his bedroom. All the strength had oozed from his weary frame, and his senses were confused and blurred. Stumblingly he reached his couch. Here he fell forward, his strained eyes closed.

He slept.

The manservant came thrice in the course of the morning, tiptoeing to the door, opening it without making a sound. His master still slept; like a piece of white sculpture the weary face lay among the pillows, rigid and motionless. The servant coughed discreetly and knocked. But no sound penetrated through the wall of slumber that guarded the exhausted musician.

In the afternoon Christopher Smith came; but no movement of his could rouse Handel from a sleep of such profound exhaustion. Christopher Smith and the manservant, who guessed nothing of the struggle and the victory, were seized with alarm, lest their master should have had another stroke.

Stefan Zweig

When, toward evening, attempts to awaken Handel were still fruitless, Smith went for the doctor.

The latter had gone fishing on the bank of the Thames and was not pleased at being recalled to professional harness. But when he heard that it was Handel who needed his services, he bundled his fishing tackle together and went home to fetch the requisites for a bloodletting.

At length the gig with the two men drove to Brook Street. The servant was on the doorstep; he waved his arms to them and shouted, "The master has got up. With a tremendous appetite! He has eaten half a ham, has drunk four pints of beer, and is clamoring for more."

They found Handel sitting in fine fettle at the groaning board. Just as he had slept the clock round and more to make up for the sleeplessness of three weeks, so was he now eating like Gargantua as if to restore, in one huge meal, all the energy he had expended during a long spell of creative activity. The instant he caught sight of the physician he began to laugh uproariously, peal after peal, without ceasing.

Smith remembered that, while engaged in his great task, the composer had not even smiled, his expression being one of tension and wrath. Now the stored-up merriment burst forth.

"May the devil fly away with me!" exclaimed Dr. Jenkins. "What's got you, man?"

Handel continued to laugh, with sparkling eyes. Then, growing serious at last, he slowly rose to his feet and strode to the harpsichord. At first his hands moved soundlessly over the keys. Half turning, he smiled enigmatically and began, as if in jest, to intone the recitative: "Behold! I tell you a mystery."

His fingers ran away with him. Forgetting self and auditors, he became immersed in creation. He sang as he played the concluding chorus. Hitherto he had heard it as if in a dream, the composer's dream; but now he was fully conscious.

"O Death, where is thy sting?"

Yes, where was Death's sting? That idea was what he felt filled with, now that Life's ardor had been renewed. Uplifting his voice, he imagined himself to be the chorus and went on playing and singing till he reached the "Amen! Amen! Amen!" So mightily did he throw himself into the music that the room seemed almost to burst with sound.

Dr. Jenkins looked on bemused. When Handel had finished, he muttered, "Never have I heard the like of this. You're possessed of the devil, you know."

A cloud obscured Handel's face. He, too, was alarmed at the scope of the work and the wonder that he had wrought as if in sleep. Humility overpowered him. With hanging head he whispered, so that the others could barely hear the words:

"I think, rather, that God has visited me."

Stefan Zweig
1881–1942

Austrian biographer, novelist, essayist, and playwright, Zweig is best known for his insightful psychological biographies of Balzac, Dickens, Dostoyevsky, and Queen Mary of Scotland.

Author Unknown

HERMEDA
SINGS A CAROL

The children sang, that cold and lovely Christmas Eve, outside every home with a candle in the window. When there were no more lighted windows, the music ceased and the children, one by one, returned home.

But little Hermeda, almost home, stopped suddenly in disbelief—a lighted window! What should she do?

Let your light so shine before men, that they may see your
good works, and glorify your Father, which is in heaven.
(Matthew 5:16)

Christmas came to the little town of Delcazette in many beautiful
ways. There was the big, stately fir tree that proudly stood in the
public square. Its tapering top disappeared into the very heavens.
At least the children thought so, for try hard as they would, they
could never see the topmost branches.

Then there were the gaily dressed shop windows, each display-
ing some Christmas novelty or some Christmas goody. Holly
wreaths hung from the brass knockers on the door of each little
cottage, and friendly pine branches arched the oval-top doorways.

But the most beautiful Christmas custom of Delcazette was the
placing of tall white candles in the windows. On Christmas Eve
all the children would gather at the little stone church nestled
snugly at the foot of the hill. From there they would travel from
cottage to cottage and sing their joyous Christmas carols beneath
every window in which was placed a lighted candle.

It was late on Christmas Eve. All day long the spotless snowflakes had noiselessly tumbled down through the chilled December air. The sleeping trees and bushes seemed to be wrapped in
a fleecy white blanket to keep them warm. The sky was like a
mantle of soft blue satin studded with sparkling rhinestones.

As the children made their way from cottage to cottage, they
filled the air with sweet childish notes of joy and praise to God
for sending the precious Baby Jesus. Their eyes twinkled merrily,
reflecting their happiness within.

One by one the candles were extinguished. That meant those
inside had heard the carols and would continue their own songs
of praise while the children traveled to the next cottage.

"How soon the night is over!" Frayer Hozen sighed. Then to the choir of children gathered about him he said, "See! The windows are all darkened. We have sung our last carol until the morning services."

"How still it is," Franz said in an awed tone, as if afraid lest he would disturb the beautiful peace that held them fast. Even the wind seemed reverently hushed.

"Just as if Baby Jesus were right here among us," added Merleen as she glanced up at the starry heavens.

"And so He is!" exclaimed the old singing master. "Now let each one hurry home. The hour is getting late, and your parents will begin to worry. It has been another beautiful Christmas Eve. How proud I am of my children's choir!"

A gentle smile lighted his thin, wrinkled face as he watched the children disappear in every direction amid the gay, happy shouts of "Merry Christmas, Frayer Hozen! Merry Christmas!"

Hermeda hurried down the deserted street alone. She had left the other girls and boys a square behind, when she had to turn off the main street. Soon she would pass the glen, and then she would be home! They would be waiting for her—her mother and father and older brothers. They would be waiting for her to sing carols for them. Then Father would take his Bible from the mantel shelf, and when they were all seated around the stone fireplace facing the crackling logs and blazing embers, he would read to them the Christmas story. Then Mother would bring from the kitchen a platter heaped with all sorts of Christmas delicacies— cookies and spice cakes and gingerbread figures and nuts and pudding. In her excitement, Hermeda began to run. She was so eager to get home. It was Christmas Eve! It was blessed Christmas Eve! She tossed back her head and took a deep breath of the crisp, clean air. Suddenly she stopped. Her eyes became as big and bright as the stars twinkling overhead. A candle! There still burned a candle! A cold, numb feeling gripped her. They had forgotten to carol beneath one window! Then she chilled again as she realized the candle was burning in the window of Machelle Brunn's home.

At first, she thought she was mistaken. It couldn't be! It just couldn't be! Why, Machelle Brunn never went to church. She never went anywhere, in fact. "The villagers are dull and stupid," so she had declared long ago. Most of them rented their farms from her, so she lived all alone in the big stone house on top of the hill. She had laughed the many times Frayer Hozen had suggested that she come to church for the Christmas Day services or that the children might come and carol for her on Christmas Eve. She even laughed at the minister and told him not to bother her with such "foolishness."

Hermeda scarcely breathed as she stared at the flickering candle flame. *She would hurry home,* she thought. *She would ask her brothers—Markhem and Stephen and Karl—to come with her.* She turned quickly and then stopped again. No. She could not do that. Machelle Brunn had been very unkind to them. It was over a fence they had been repairing at the edge of their orchard. Machelle Brunn had declared they were using some of her wood, and she had said untrue and unkind words to them. No. It would not be wise to ask her brothers to go to the top of the hill with her. They would not understand why she wanted to go.

She glanced again at the flickering candle. How lonely it looked away up there. How unhappy it seemed! Just as if it were beckoning and pleading and begging someone to come and bring the Christ child to the big, cold, dismal stone house. *Perhaps,* thought Hermeda, *Machelle Brunn was lonely this Christmas Eve. Perhaps she placed the candle in the window as a sign that she wanted to be one of them and worship with them in the very church her own grandfather had built so long ago.* She would go herself. She would carol all alone outside the window. She could do it. Had she not sung all alone to the whole congregation many times?

Hermeda felt so small and so unimportant as she stood in the shadows beneath the window of the big stone house. How quiet and forlorn and even unhappy the house seemed! *What should she sing?* she thought. Then her face beamed. *The First Noel,* of course! Truly, it was the first Noel sung beneath that window since Machelle Brunn became mistress of the old stone manor.

As Hermeda sang, she kept her eyes on the candle, but no face appeared above its glow. Again and again she sang, but still the flame flickered and beckoned and pleaded. *How strange,* she thought! *Surely Machelle Brunn could hear her!* She hesitated a moment, and then, standing on her tiptoes, she peered in at the window.

At first it was hard to see anything, for the room was in darkness save for the waning candlelight. Then Hermeda noticed the candle was not on the windowsill, as she had supposed, but on a little table pushed against it. Hermeda pressed her face closer to the cold glass. Then she scarcely breathed as she saw Machelle Brunn sitting with her head buried in her outstretched arms on top of the table. Instantly Hermeda knew there was something wrong. Machelle Brunn was ill. There was no time to be lost. She must go to her and help her.

Hermeda found that the paneled front door opened as she turned the knob. A big grandfather clock ticked sadly in the corner of the quiet hall as if grieving for lack of company. But Hermeda scarcely noticed the stillness of the rooms as she hurried to Machelle Brunn. She shook the figure gently and called her by name, but she made no reply. Hermeda glanced about the shadowed room. If only she knew where the kitchen was. She could get some cold water for Machelle Brunn's forehead. That would help, she knew. She glanced out of the window. Then her eyes sparkled. The very thing! She could use the snow, which lay thick even on the wide stone porch.

When Machelle Brunn felt the cold snow on her fevered fore-head, she opened her eyes.

"Are you all right now?" Hermeda asked quietly. "Do you feel better?"

Machelle Brunn slowly sat erect and gazed at the little girl standing before her.

"Who are you?" she asked in a faltering tone.

Hermeda smiled, a soft, cheery, radiant smile that seemed to brighten the room.

"I'm Hermeda Vannest," she said quietly. "I saw your candle on my way home. I thought we had forgotten to carol to you."

"To carol to me!" Machelle Brunn repeated in a bewildered tone. "To carol to me!"

"Yes," came the quiet reply. "You see, the children's choir was caroling all evening. I was almost home when I happened to see the candle in your window. I thought we had forgotten you."

Machelle Brunn's face seemed softer. Almost kind. "And so you came alone," she said slowly as if trying to realize what had happened. "You came all by yourself! But why?" she added quickly, leaning forward eagerly.

"The candle seemed to be calling to me. It looked so lonely and so sad burning all alone up here," answered Hermeda, look-ing into the sad eyes of Machelle Brunn. "I thought perhaps the candle meant you had changed your mind and wanted to be one of us."

For a moment the tired, lonely Machelle Brunn sat quietly, gazing steadily at Hermeda. The candlelight added a soft glow to the child's cheeks and the few stray curls that escaped from beneath her little red knit tam.

"Perhaps you are right," she said at last. "Perhaps I changed my mind long ago and have been waiting for just such a chance to tell everyone. I was on my way upstairs with the candle in my hand, and suddenly I felt faint. I thought I would sit down for a moment until I felt better. I just happened to be close to this chair and table near the window. And you saw my candlelight," she continued in a strangely soft tone for Machelle Brunn. "And you thought I had placed a candle in my window to beckon the children carolers!" A happy light shone in her tired eyes. It softened the many deep lines in her face. "And you came and you sang to me! Sing to me once again, Hermeda. Sing for me just one Christmas carol! Just one more before you go home."

At the word *home,* Hermeda gave a little gasp. Gracious! She had forgotten all about going home! Hermeda looked at Machelle Brunn with excited eyes.

"Oh, I must hurry!" she exclaimed. "They will be waiting for me. They will be worried lest something has happened! They will be gathered around the fireplace waiting for me to sing Christmas carols for them. Then Father will read the Christmas story from the Bible, and Mother will bring forth her Christmas goodies, and we shall all feast! Machelle Brunn!" she suddenly exclaimed in wild excitement as she moved closer to the elderly lady. "Come home with me! Spend Christmas Eve with us in our cottage!"

A bright light shone in Machelle Brunn's eyes. *Christmas Eve with a happy family! Christmas Eve in a cottage!*

"I will!" she said with a shaking voice. "I've waited so long for this! Come, Hermeda, I'll get my wrap, and we will start at once!"

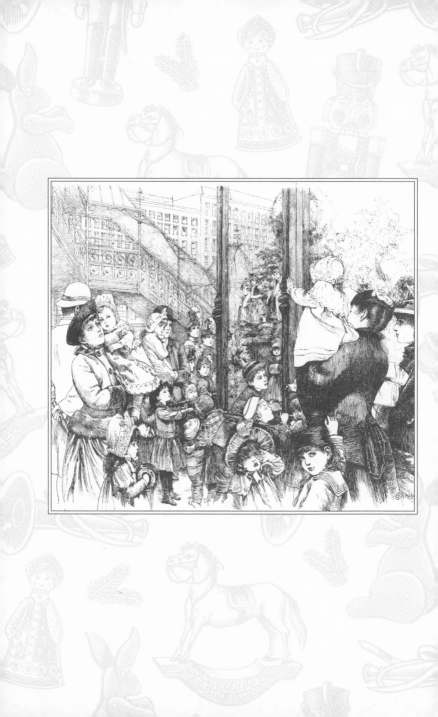

Marguerite Brunner

THERE IS MAGIC
IN BELIEVING

Christmas was coming and five-year-old Susie had set her heart on getting Betsy, the big doll in Dorsey's Drugstore window. But the price was an impossible twenty-four dollars. To her struggling mother, it might as well have been one thousand dollars. Even worse, Susie took the matter over Santa's head to God.

And then just before Christmas, someone else bought the doll. How could Susie's mother possibly face her on Christmas morning?

Susie never doubted for a minute that the big doll in Dorsey's Drugstore window would belong to her on Christmas morning. Sandy, my ten-year-old, said Susie visited the window every morning after I left for the hospital, where I worked as a nurse's aid.

The doll cost twenty-four dollars. To me, that seemed like all the money in the world, but to Susie, who was just five, it didn't seem like much at all. The two and the four didn't seem beyond the realm of her imagination. She'd often had two cents and sometimes four. The dollar sign meant nothing.

I was washing dishes after supper when Sandy told me about Susie's visit that day. "She calls the doll Betsy, Mom," she said, drying a dish. "This morning she walked up to the window and said, 'Don't forget to tell Santa Claus that I'm the one who wants to adopt you. It would be awful tragic if he made a mistake and left you to one of my sisters or that kid next door. They just wouldn't 'reciate you at all!'"

Sandy noticed the tears in my eyes. "What are we going to do, Mom?"

"Oh, something will turn up," I assured her, forcing a lightness I didn't feel. "We have ten days till Christmas."

But the week before Christmas arrived, and there were no prospects of anything extra. The kids strung up colored strips of paper on a string behind the kitchen door. Each morning it was a mad scramble to see who could get there first and pull off the paper for that day. Even two-year-old Mike could count the remaining papers and tell you how many days were left till Santa would come.

That week the snow fell, blanketing the city with a fluffy white coat. One day the heavy snow snarled traffic so that the busses couldn't run and I couldn't get across town to work. Sandy, though only ten, knew how worried I was. We kept few secrets from each other.

"They won't pay you for today?" she asked, frowning. "What will we do?"

I looked down at the worried, freckled face and thought sadly, *You're growing up too fast. It's my fault, but what can I do?*

"We'll manage," I assured her. "And think of all the fun we can have!"

"At least we saved Mrs. Brown's baby-sitting money this week," she said cheerfully. "I'm glad I could help us save that much."

Since school was out for the holidays, Sandy had become my sitter, and she took care of the young ones like an old hand.

The children loved having me home. We popped corn over the gas flame on the stove, and, with much persuasion, Susie talked me into trudging through the knee-high snow to the corner drugstore to visit Betsy.

"This is ridiculous," I told her as we tried to make a path through the snow. "Susie, that doll is out of the question. Please, honey, believe me, when I tell you that bringing toys to our five kids at Christmas is quite a drain on Santa's pocketbook. I doubt that he has more than twenty-four dollars to spend on the lot of you. Please, honey," I begged, trying to keep up, "don't set your heart on getting her, for I'm afraid you'll be disappointed Christmas morning."

Susie laughed and squeezed my hand. "Don't you worry, Mommy," she said reassuringly. "Betsy and me have a 'greement, and she's gonna tell Santa that she don't want to live with anybody but me, and I know he'll bring her. Just you wait and see."

What can you tell a five-year-old who ends every prayer with, "And dear God, don't forget Betsy. When I get her, I'll take her to church every week—if it don't rain."

Susie broke loose as we neared the drugstore. She tried to run but fell in the snow. She got up laughing. "Isn't snow the nicest thing that falls out of the sky?"

I recalled another snowy Christmas week a year ago, when my husband, John, had come face-to-face with himself. I remembered the night I'd come home from the hospital to find the apartment in darkness. John had spent the light money on drinks at the corner bar, and the light company had cut off the electricity three days before Christmas.

I remembered how the children had huddled around the only candle in the house and watched my face. I could still hear Sandy telling the young ones that Mother would fix it and they mustn't cry.

I'd always made a practice of not scolding John in front of the children, for intoxicated though he might be, he was never cross with them. They used to say, "Daddy's sick again."

After the children were in bed and asleep, I faced him over the dying candle. "I'm sorry," he cried. "I must have been out of my mind. Why do you put up with me? You and the kids would be better off without me."

For the first time, I agreed with him. "I think you're right," I told him, almost calmly. "We can't go on this way much longer."

I remembered how hurt he'd looked and how I'd wanted to reassure him, to say I hadn't meant what I'd said, but the words wouldn't come. I could feel the soft touch of material under my hands. I'd had a rush order of draperies to be finished for the drapery shop before Christmas, and we needed that money so desperately, but without lights I couldn't sew.

"I'm going to get out and stay out, until I can straighten myself out," he had said slowly. "When I come back, I'll have this thing licked."

And while the children slept, he'd slipped out into the softly falling snow, and I'd not heard a word from him in the whole year. For all I knew, he might be dead.

That night I had guiltily felt almost relieved that he was gone. One less mouth to feed, and I wouldn't have to hide the grocery money anymore. John had spent every cent he could get his hands on for drinks. The only work he'd done in over a year had been at the corner bar, sweeping up the floor or taking out empty beer kegs, and more often than not, they'd paid him off with drinks.

It had been that way since his accident. Before, he'd been a house painter and a good one. He had provided well for us, but then he'd fallen from the ladder and hurt his back. Although the doctors discharged him, the pain persisted so much that he'd often cry out. Then he began to drink. Just one or two drinks in the beginning so he could sleep. Then gradually, as the pain became more intense, so did the drinking, until he was never without it.

At first he was apologetic about not working. Tomorrow he'd feel better and go out and get a job, but tomorrow never came, and five hungry children continued to eat. Because I refused to sign papers to have him committed to a state hospital, the social worker who called on us refused to recommend welfare help.

"First you must help yourselves," she told me, and I lay awake nights, worrying about what would happen to the children. I remembered cases I'd read about where the children had been taken away from their parents and put in foster homes. Determined that this would never happen to mine, I got that job at the hospital and did part-time sewing for the drapery shop.

I sewed rather well and loved the pretty, expensive material that Mr. Long delivered to the apartment. Last year for Christmas he'd given me enough material for draperies for the apartment. But I'd needed the money worse, so I made it into draperies for one of the nurses at the hospital. She'd paid well, and the extra money helped a lot, since the light company required a deposit when they turned the lights back on.

As Susie and I walked through the snow, I kept thinking about John, wondering where he was and how many beers he could buy with the money he had in his pocket. He had been so far gone before he left that he thought of money in terms of drinks. "I've got only six beers to my name," he'd say.

When we reached the drugstore window, Susie ran ahead of me. "Betsy," she cried out, "I've brought Mommy today. You'll like my mommy!"

Through tear-filled eyes, I could have sworn I saw the doll smile!

"How do you do, Betsy?" I asked, for this wasn't the first time I'd joined the children when they talked to their imaginary friends.

"Betsy says you're nice, and she likes you very much," Susie said, hugging my arm.

I moved closer to the window, hoping not to attract the attention of any passersby. "I think we'd better have a little talk, Betsy," I said for Susie's benefit. "Susie wants you very much. She talks of little else; but we have five little ones at home, and I'm afraid you wouldn't like living with us. Now, Mike is only two, and he'd pull your hair, maybe even poke your eyes out. Judy is three and loves to scrub the very skin off dolls. The apartment is small, and we'd have no place for you to sleep, and there'd be no money for fine clothes like you're wearing. Won't you please tell Susie that you'd rather go live in a big house where you could live like a lady?"

Susie listened intently. Suddenly she broke out laughing. "Oh, Mommy, Betsy and me settled that weeks ago. Betsy says she doesn't mind sleeping on the floor beside my bed, and I told her you'd make her some dresses out of scraps you have left over from the drapes. She thinks that would be wonderful. And if Mike pulled her hair or tried to poke her eyes out, she'd just bite him. She's got real, live teeth, you know!"

Completely defeated, I took her arm. "Tell Betsy good-bye. We'd better get home and make lunch."

Many times that week I wished I could turn the clock back two years. I wished desperately that John, sober and his old smiling self, were there.

Three days before Christmas, as I prepared an elderly patient for surgery, I spotted some money lying in the drawer of her bedside table. From the size of the roll of bills, I was positive that there were at least twenty-five dollars. My hands trembled as I helped her into the hospital gown.

"You say you have five children?" she asked, as I tied the strings in back of the gown. "I had nine, and every one of them was a blessing. When you get old like me, you'll understand what I mean."

I hardly heard what she was saying. I kept hearing Susie's voice at the drugstore window. I'd never stolen a thing in my life, but here, close enough to touch, was the answer to my little girl's prayer.

The nurse came and gave the old lady a hypo. I hovered over her as she became drowsy. When they came and rolled her out, I was to change her bed and make ready for her return. It would be easy! Nobody need ever know. And Susie would have her doll!

I made the bed automatically. I'd made hundreds of beds; I could do it with my eyes closed. When I stood on the side where the table was, I slipped my hand into the drawer and quickly gathered up the bills and tucked them into my uniform. The money burned like a hot coal.

I felt trembly all over. Had someone seen me? Breathlessly I crossed the room and walked furtively down the hall. Would the old lady miss the money today? I was filled with guilty anxiety that I'd never felt before. Fortunately I finished my hours before she returned from surgery.

On my way home I got off the bus at the drugstore. My heart was pounding in my throat as I crossed the street and ran through piled snow to Dorsey's window. Suddenly the big empty space loomed up at me. Betsy was gone! I couldn't believe it. Silently I prayed, *Please, God, not this. Not now, when I have the money.*

I hurried inside and asked for the manager. "That big doll you had in the window—where is she?"

"Oh," the man laughed, "we finally sold her. I knew she was much too expensive for this neighborhood, but I let the salesman talk me into buying one. I thought for sure I was stuck with it, but this morning the girl did sell it."

I felt suddenly empty inside. "Do you think I can find another like her?" I asked weakly. "My little girl has her heart set on that particular doll."

"You might try the department stores," the manager said sympathetically. "If you'll wait a minute, I'll get the model number and the name of the manufacturer."

Armed with a dozen dimes, I sat in the phone booth and called all the department stores and discount houses. Nobody had a model 219. Sick at heart, I left the drugstore and started for home. How could I ever explain to Susie? Five was such a young age to meet such a big disappointment.

That night I couldn't sleep. The thirty-one dollars I'd stolen burned in my conscience. The full impact of what I'd done left me sick with fear. Suppose someone came and wanted to search my house? Suppose they were just waiting for me to come to work tomorrow to arrest me?

The doll was gone. Perhaps that was God's way of punishing me for what I'd done. Now Susie would know that believing was not enough. At the tender age of five, she'd know that life was hard and ruthless and that God doesn't always answer the prayers of even little girls.

"John! John!" I cried into my pillow. "Where are you? We need you so much."

I wasn't due at the hospital until nine, but I left the house at seven. I *had* to give the money back. I awakened Sandy and told her I had to go early and for her to make breakfast for the others.

Outside the hospital my steps lagged. If they arrested me, what would become of my children?

I pushed the money inside my glove and headed straight for Mrs. Johnson's room. She was eating breakfast and looking very well for a patient who had undergone surgery only yesterday.

"Good morning," she said brightly. "You're early this morning."

I felt my face burning, and I could not meet her eyes.

"I have your money here," I told her, taking it out of my glove.

"Oh, you're such a considerate person," she beamed. "I knew you must have taken it for safekeeping. I meant to ask you to keep it for me. Thank you very much."

I felt terrible. Did she really think I had taken it to keep for her, or was she just trying to make it easier for me?

When I went to the locker room to put my coat away, I felt suddenly lighthearted. Thank God, the doll was gone. I must have been out of my mind, thinking I could make a wrong into a right. Somehow I'd make Susie understand that Christmas is for giving, not receiving.

Christmas Eve fell on my regular day off. I'd been working one of my days off for two weeks, so that I might have both the day before Christmas and Christmas Day with the children. That morning the children scurried from their beds at an early hour. The last strip of paper was snatched from the string behind the door.

"Santa comes tonight!" they squealed, scampering through the apartment.

"Betsy comes tonight!" laughed Susie. "I can't wait for tonight. Betsy's already been picked up by Santa Claus. He got her two days ago."

Some of the old weariness crept back over me. I got up and started breakfast. How could I tell her? What would I say? I started, seeking each word as I went, feeling my way.

"Children," I began, "tonight will be Christmas Eve. It's the time of year we must think of giving, not receiving. The Wise Men and the shepherds came to visit the Baby Jesus, bringing gifts. For that reason, people down through the ages have given gifts.

"Now there are many poor children. Some, whose mothers and fathers are sick or dead, will not receive gifts tonight, because Santa Claus has to have money to buy the lovely presents he brings children. We are very lucky that Mommy has a job and we're able to give Santa Claus some money for toys, but I think it would be thoughtful if each of you wrote Santa a note and asked him to take one of your toys to a poor child, who otherwise might not get anything at all. What do you say?"

You could have heard a pin drop. Each child sat in silent thought. Breathlessly, I waited. The speech hadn't been for the others, only for Susie. There was no other way I could think of to handle it.

"You mean I ought to let Betsy go live with a poor kid?" she piped up, tears filling her eyes. "You said she ought to live with rich people when you talked to her at the drugstore."

"Why don't we just leave it up to Santa Claus to take whatever toy he thinks best for a poor kid or maybe a child that is sick? Just getting a fine toy might help make a sick child get well real fast."

"Oh, that's different," Susie said, scrambling for a tablet and pencil. "I just know he won't take Betsy—we belong."

"But if he does," I said, trying to sound casual, "you won't cry? You'll think about some poor, sick little girl, who woke up Christmas morning and found Betsy and got all well, because she had someone to love?"

"I guess so," she said slowly, but I knew I hadn't convinced her at all.

By eight o'clock that night, the children were all ready for bed. Prayers had been said and each had climbed into bed. The time had finally come. The radio announced that Santa Claus had just left the North Pole for his yearly flight around the world. There were hushed whispers from bed to bed.

Sandy came into the living room where I sat. "She's going to be sick in the morning, isn't she, Mom?" she asked, cuddling up beside me on the sofa.

"I'm afraid so. The doll was gone when I went to get her. I really tried, but someone had already bought it, and there wasn't another anywhere."

"Would it help if I prayed for a doll for Susie? You used to say that if we prayed for something and it was good for us and we really believed we'd get it, God would send it to us."

I felt my heart being twisted inside of me. "Yes," I said brokenly, "it will help to pray. It always helps to pray. But maybe the doll isn't good for Susie. She has to learn that she can't have everything she wants."

"That's just it," Sandy said, kissing me good night, "she never really wanted anything before. This is the first time she really cared for anything."

"Run along to bed. I can manage alone, and I have lots to do."

When Sandy left the room, I began sobbing like a baby. I couldn't stop. A doll was such an insignificant thing, but the heartbreak of my little girl was too much. I couldn't bear to think about the morning.

I lowered the blinds and set about pulling the presents from the hall closet. There was another small doll for Susie. She didn't compare with the elegance of Betsy, but maybe she could help ease the disappointment. There was a truck for Mike and a fire engine for Tommy and a doll for Judy, a washable doll. She'd enjoy scrubbing the soft rubber skin. There were skates for Sandy. She would have loved a bike, but she knew it was out of the question. *Bless Sandy,* I thought, arranging the toys. *She was a blessing, as the old lady had said.*

When I finished, I turned out the lights and went to bed. Almost immediately, I fell into an exhausted sleep.

It was scarcely daybreak when I was awakened by the delighted squeals of the children. "Wake up, Mommy," Susie called in an excited voice. "Come, say good morning to Betsy!"

Startled out of my sleep, I sat up in bed and stared in disbelief. There stood Susie with the beautiful doll from Dorsey's Drugstore.

"Where on earth did she come from?" I stammered.

"Oh, Santa Claus brought her, just like I said he would. He brought Sandy a bike and the boys tricycles and Judy a doll with high-heeled shoes."

I sprang out of bed and stumbled into the front room that had been transformed into a toy fairyland—magnificent, beautiful toys! The things I'd bought seemed small and insignificant by comparison.

This was truly a Christmas miracle! Under the tree I found a big box with my name on it—wrapped in lovely paper, tied with beautiful ribbons. As I nervously fumbled with the wrappings, a card fell out:

"I was close enough to touch you and Susie in front of Dorsey's Drugstore, but I couldn't muster up the nerve. After thinking of little else this last year, now I am afraid there might not be a place for me. Is there? If so, please drop a ribbon out the window." The card was signed, "Santa Claus."

Happily I tore the bow off my gift and hurried to open the window. The children watched me with amazement as I dropped the ribbons to the ground atop the white snow.

"Why did you do that?" Sandy asked.

"Because somebody special is out there waiting for a sign from us. When he sees the ribbons, he'll come home again."

"Daddy! Daddy!" Sandy cried, heading for the door. "Daddy's come home!" All the children began to run down the steps to meet their father.

The miracle of that Christmas will never leave me. Anytime I feel doubts, I remember how the faith of my five-year-old and the prayers of my ten-year-old brought a miracle.

Gillette Jones

THE
CHRISTMAS ROOM

Joan's family was the wealthiest in town, while Barbara's was one of the poorest. But one thing Joan's family didn't *have*—a Christmas room. So she came over to see the "Christmas room" at Barbara's house. Would she ridicule it? Would she sneer? Would she laugh?

When I arrived at my daughter's on Christmas Eve, the children ran to the door with shouts and kisses, giving me a greeting that would make any grandma glad. Then, struggling with my bags, they took me to the guest room. I stopped short at the door of the room, staring at the sign that hung there. In red and green crayon it read The Christmas Room. My throat ached for a moment, as I remembered. . . .

Our daughter Barbara was only nine when she began to realize that we were quite poor. In Barbara's class there was one girl who took special delight in tormenting her. It was an odd friendship between Barbara and Joan. Joan came from the wealthiest family in town—one of the few that hadn't been affected by the Depression. Joan was outgoing, Barbara quiet and shy.

Joan was all ups and downs: one minute befriending Barbara, treating her to candy, giving her a toy—the next, bragging extravagantly, teaching Barbara to be ashamed of our house.

We kept hoping Barbara would overcome her shyness and make other friends, but she continued to tag after Joan, in spite of the hurts she suffered. Joan, delighting in Barbara's vulnerability, kept her on a string at her side.

Christmas was coming. I knew ours would be a lean one indeed, unless we used a great deal of imagination. Early in November we started planning. Barbara helped me look for recipes that were inexpensive. We colored Epsom salt and put it in pretty bottles for bath salts for her grandmothers. We took scraps of velvet and transformed ordinary boxes into jewel boxes for the grandfathers' stickpins. We dreamed up pincushions that looked like miniature hats and pot holders in the shape of teapots. We spent hours in the little spare room laughing at each new touch of imagination.

The lumpy old daybed became littered with gay scraps of paper as we cut pictures from last year's Christmas cards to decorate our packages. We had a wonderful time together.

One day in early December, Barbara went to Joan's house after school and returned looking sad.

"What's the trouble?" I asked her.

"Oh, nothing."

"There is something," I said. "Is Joan bragging again?"

"It's not that. I'm sort of used to that." She hesitated, then said, "Mom, I told a fib today."

I was thankful she found it disturbing, at least.

"But that Joan!" Her voice had an edge of bitterness. "She's always talking about the Blue Room and the company that sleeps there. Today she asked me, 'Where does *your* company sleep?'"

We never had overnight company. It was hard enough to feed ourselves on Jim's meager salary. And our homely little spare room was just that. It had two old pieces of furniture in it—a daybed and a wobbly end table.

Barbara went on, "I told Joan we don't have much company, and her eyebrow went up. Mom, I just couldn't stand that look again. So I told her, 'We have something you don't. We have a Christmas room.'"

Her feet shuffled. "I didn't mean to fib, but you should have seen how surprised she looked. I never saw Joan stuck before. She really didn't know what to say."

"But, dear, you weren't fibbing," I said. "We *do* have a Christmas room. But if it will make it more official, we'll make a sign for the door."

She brightened. "Oh, could we?"

"We'll do it today."

The sign was barely dry and hung when Joan arrived. She had rarely come to our house, always preferring to take Barbara to her house where there were lots of toys to play with. Now she stood at our door asking to see the Christmas room.

Barbara looked at me. "May I show her?"

"I guess so," I answered. "If everything is wrapped, that is."
Barbara went to check on the condition of packages, while I
explained to Joan, "The room is full of surprises, and we can't let
any secrets out."

Barbara hurried back into the room. "It's OK."

I held my breath. Joan would see only a small dingy room with
a cracked ceiling and a homemade sign on the door. She would
not see or feel the special qualities that room held for us.

They were gone so long, I finally went to the hallway and
peered in. Joan was looking at our crèche—paper figures we had
cut and stood on the end table.

"We have china figures," she said. "Imported."

I started to speak, but just then Joan moved to the packages
that were lined up on the daybed. She touched them one by one,
lingering over the one with the paper sled on it. That was one
Barbara had done from colored paper. She had filled the sled with
miniature packages.

Joan turned to Barbara. "We don't have surprises. I always
know everything."

"How?" Barbara asked. "Do you peek?"

Joan shook her head. "They ask what I want—and I get it."

Barbara said impulsively, "I'll give you a surprise."

Joan shrugged. "If you want."

Barbara nodded solemnly, before I could stop her.

During the next week, we tossed ideas about, rejecting them
all. There seemed nothing we could give this child who had everything. At last, we settled somewhat apprehensively on giving
her one afternoon a week at our house, helping to make surprises. I wasn't at all sure she'd think it was a present.

She did come, however. The first time, we made cookies and
wrapped some for her mother. The next week, it was fancy
matchboxes for her father. The week before Christmas, Barbara

gave her a box to open. Joan tore at the paper, but when she had the lid off, she didn't know what the contents were. Barbara looked disappointed, and I added, "It's corn—for popping."

I tried to force gaiety into my words. It wasn't easy when Barbara's face said plainly that she wished we had given Joan something different, something better.

When the corn was popped, Joan tasted it and remarked, "I could never make this. It's too messy for our house."

I glanced quickly at Barbara, but she was busy showing Joan how the corn could be dyed pink or blue with food coloring.

"Later, we'll string it for the Christmas tree," she explained.

Joan worked at it, occasionally holding up the colorful string without comment. I couldn't tell whether she was having fun. But suddenly I knew I wanted her to—very much.

"They'll never hang this on our tree," she snorted.

"Would you like to come hang it on our tree?" I ventured.

Her sudden tears alarmed me. *"Could I?"* she asked. "I can never help trim ours. I might break things." She pushed back her chair. "I'd better go now."

She got her coat and hat quickly, but in the Christmas room she had a long moment of hesitation about whether to actually take home the things she'd made for her parents. At last she decided. She picked them up.

We watched her leave, clutching her small surprises. Both of us hoped that her parents would not laugh at her offerings.

Barbara turned big eyes toward me and whispered, "I used to be jealous of her."

That was long ago when Barbara was very young. It had been a childhood thing, important at the time, but long forgotten, I'd thought. Now once again I stood facing a sign on a door that read The Christmas Room.

I stepped inside, into a pleasant room with pale blue walls and crisp curtains—not at all like our homely old spare room. On the windowseat there were packages wrapped with special touches of childish imagination. The children ran to them.

"I made this!" Ronnie cried proudly.

"You're going to love mine, Grandma," Paula shouted.

There was no financial need for Barbara to do with her children what we had done—but I was so glad she had. She'd been young that year of the Christmas room, yet even then, she must have known that a Christmas room is a room for people, for thoughts of others, a room in the heart.

Joseph Leininger Wheeler

LEGACY

Just what is a legacy? Is it a masterpiece created by a great painter or sculptor? Is it a villa by the sea? Is it a treasure chest of rare gems? Is it stocks and bonds worth millions?

Or could it be something entirely different?

It was cold and foggy that bleak December day on the Oregon coast. But inside my aunt's farmhouse living room it was cheery, and a hot fire crackled in the big black iron stove. On the mantel was a stack of Christmas cards and letters, and in a corner a small Christmas tree.

Suddenly, around the corner stalked Mr. Tibbs, a proud old tomcat of venerable years and uncertain ancestry. But lack of pedigree had never bothered Mr. Tibbs. In fact, he reveled in his mongrel Americanism. *He* would establish the dynasty.

Called upon by my aunt to perform for me, Mr. Tibbs leisurely responded in his own good time, letting me know he condescended to do so, not because I was in any respect worthy of it, but because he owed my aunt one of his royal favors. Old as he was, he hesitated before wheezing his way to the stool top, licked his chops at the cheese my aunt held high above him, then stood up tall on his back legs to claim the prize, yet never for a moment losing his dignity.

After Mr. Tibbs had paid his dues, he descended from the stool and swaggered out.

In the quiet moments that followed, I wondered: *Do I dare bring it up . . . again? Surely, if she had been receptive to my plea, she would have responded long ere this. And, for good measure, my uncle hadn't responded either—and now he lies in his grave up on that misty green hill overlooking the valley. Perhaps . . . I'd just better forget it for now.* So I said nothing and only leaned back into the softness of the couch, dozy because of the alder wood fire.

I was a boy again . . . and my heart was leaping within me because I knew we were nearing the ranch. The first gate loomed ahead, and Dad's Ford slowed and stopped so I could get out. This had always been *my* job! The long wooden bar slid back, and the heavy gate lifted and opened at last; then I stood there holding it while the Ford chugged past me and stopped.

Ever so slowly, for I was ever so small, I struggled across the road, that balky gate fighting me all the way. After reinserting the bar, I ran up to the car for the best part of all: riding on the running board to the other size of Frazzi's vineyard. Some days we'd drive up to the Frazzi house, and Mrs. Frazzi, large of girth, dark of complexion, poor with her English, and robust with her belly laugh, would throw her plump arms around me, brag about how I had grown, and tow me over to the always-overflowing cookie jar.

But not today. . . . Down I leaped for the second gate, also of heavy wood. It too a struggle, and resisting every inch, squawking all the way. Once again the Ford rolled past and stopped. Once again I got on the running board.

The next gate, of metal pipe and wire mesh, was easier. Overhead, I could hear the wind in the pines; occasionally, we'd see a deer bounding through the manzanita, madrone, and buck brush bushes. Today the road was dusty, sometimes there would be snow on it instead.

I jumped on the running board again, and as we jolted our way ever higher up the mountain, my heart was beating so turbulently it threatened to leap out of me. At last, the big maple tree and the clearing. Thousands of apple trees to our left, and just ahead at the top of the crest was the walled home of the self-anointed "Old Man of the Mountain," Grandpa Rollo, and his jolly wife, Grandma Ruby, who was deaf.

All the way up that last hill, Dad laid on the horn; as he swerved around to the house, there they were waving, Grandma saying over and over to Grandpa, "Wh-y-y-y, Papa!" and to each of us in turn, "You d-e-e-a-a-r soul!" Background sound provided by barking dogs.

Up there on top of the mountain, the seven-hundred-acre

ranch stretched away, to my childish eyes, to forever. I would explore it later. First of all, though, we'd go through the gate, through the evergreen tree windbreak behind the rock wall, to the little rock house in the middle. The door *always* squeaked. Inside, it was rather dark, but there on the lip of the rock fireplace were the purring cats. As often as not, one of them would be leaning against the great wicker basket of blocks.

The wind would howl and the rain would pelt, but inside that snug little cabin of a house, with so much love and laughter; with the fire in the fireplace; with the kerosene lamp's soft glow; with the fragrance of homemade bread, fresh applesauce, and cold milk just feet away; with one of the cats or kittens purring on my lap, and the blocks already stacked into dream buildings—well, it was home, it was Shangri-la.

Then, we'd hear other horns, other slammed car doors, each punctuated by "Why Papa's!" and "You dear soul's!" Then, more laughter as uncles and aunts and cousins poured into the walled enclosure.

Swirling mists blotted out the little cabin and the side house we children stayed in when we got older, with its swinging, banging doors with semiclear plastic instead of windows, and not far beyond, the outhouse with its abridged Sears catalogue and pesky wasps.

Years passed, and we flew in silver DC3s to places thousands of miles away. Places where there were bougainvillea on the patios, royal palms bowing in rainy-season winds, freshly cut stalks of bananas on our back porch, and exhausting heat.

But, every once in a blessed while, the silver birds would bring us back home, home to the three gates, the "Why Papa's!" the "You dear soul's!" the cats on the hearth, and the blocks.

Once, a new word entered my childish vocabulary. My grandfather was hauled into court by a neighboring rancher over water rights. The opposing attorney, attempting to diminish the value of Grandpa's ranch, asked the loaded question: "How much is your ranch worth?"

Grandpa's attorney, never missing a beat, stepped in and shot a question back: "Do you mean the value if it came on the real estate market? Or do you mean its *esoteric* value?" *Esoteric* was a big word for me, but after I looked it up in the dictionary and had Mom explain it, I thoroughly understood. The esoteric value was the greatest view in all the Napa Valley region, the multi-hued sunsets, the fog banks rolling in from the Pacific, the snow flocking the evergreens and apple trees, the little walled house on the mountaintop, the thoughts, the dreams . . . oh how—how could one possibly put a value on all that? Ah yes, it was easy for me to grasp the attorney's question, for children value esoterically to begin with.

A door slammed, and I was jerked out of the past and slammed into the present. I heard voices: My aunt was needed down at the barn. . . . Then there was silence again, and once again I slipped backward in time.

A number of years had passed, and Grandpa and Grandma were growing old. The winters at the top of the mountain were hard and cold. The apple business was exhausting. Then came the news: The big ranch was sold, and they were moving down the mountain to a smaller (eighty-acre) place.

The next time we went to see them, we came to their one gate only a short distance off the paved road. There was a larger compound now, surrounded by a long mesh fence, to keep the deer out. Initially, there was only a tiny cabin there, but over time Grandpa built a big beautiful brick home, a veritable palace compared to the older one! Out the broad picture windows, one could look across the valley to a small lake. There were rocks and boulders everywhere, but Grandma Ruby determined (now that the children were grown and gone, now that the apple ranch had been sold) to transform her little piece of earth into a flowering paradise.

It would prove a never-ending task, and Grandma would have to wrestle like Jacob for every blossom, for every lacy fern, for every rosebud. Now, when we honked and drove in, scattering cats and kittens in our wake, chances are we'd have to get out of the car, search out the business end of the garden hose, and tap her on the shoulder before we'd hear "Why, you dear soul!"—and looking over our shoulders, "Why, Papa!"

Then we'd haul our suitcases into the big new house. Inside, it was spotlessly clean—it was kept that way. And it was easy to do so because, to Grandma and Grandpa, the new house was too grand to live in. They compromised by installing an iron stove in the garage and moving in there. The main house was reserved for the family: all nine surviving children and throngs of grandchildren. Grandpa now did most of the cooking (the applesauce and nut bread) in the tiny little cabin, for Grandma had traded cooking for flowers. The beautiful kitchen in the main house was generally used only when company came.

When we'd come into the big house, there in the large family room was the great fireplace, and there on the hearth would be the wicker basket of blocks. There were never any other toys: just the blocks. As a child, I never really examined them or wondered how old they were—I just played with them. When my cousins wandered in, they'd plunk themselves down on the floor and play with me.

As we got older, however, the siren call of horseshoes drew us outside to where those authority figures, the men, were challenging each other, trying to beat Grandpa. To us, a rite of passage was reached when we were deemed old enough to play. Every Thanksgiving, as the clan gathered from far and near, the clang of horseshoes could be heard all day long. Except for during dinner when we all gathered around the long, groaning trestle table in the big house. Around it we saw a side of our parents we never saw anywhere else, for here they were still considered children by Grandpa and Grandma.

And how Grandpa loved to tell stories: stories like the one where my cousin Billy sidled up to Grandpa in the orchard and drawled, "G-r-a-n-d-p-a . . . I t-h-i-n-k I s-e-e a-a-a s-n-a-k-e." And, as Grandpa would tell it, he'd always counter, "Now, Billy, don't tell lies! You *know* there's no snake around today."

There'd be silence for a while, until Billy forgot about the admonition and sidled up to Grandpa saying: "G-r-a-n-d-p-a, I t-h-i-n-k I s-e-e a-a-a s-n-a-k-e," and again Grandpa would warn him not to tell lies, and again Billy would subside.

Then, Grandpa would grin as for the third time he'd hear, "G-r-a-n-d-p-a, I t-h-i-n-k I-I SEE A SNAKE!" And, no matter how many times we'd heard the story, we'd jump a foot off our chairs when Grandpa'd galvanize into frightened little boy action.

And other stories like the one about a man who used to take a shortcut home, from time to time, through a graveyard. Well, one dark and moonless night, he was walking through on the way home, and unbeknownst to him, earlier that day a new grave had been dug for a funeral the following day. Well, here he came: *pad, pad, pad,* and suddenly there was no path, and *whumpf,* he plunged into the open grave. After he got up and gathered his wits, he realized where he was and tried to climb out, but it was too deep. So he called out for help, loud and long, but no one could hear him. *Finally,* exhausted, he gave up and sat down in one corner to wait for morning.

By this time in the story, tingles would be going up our spines as we waited for "Suddenly, he heard someone coming. *Pad, pad, pad,* and *whumpf, another* man fell in!" Pausing to make sure he still had his audience, Grandpa then proceeded to tell us that the new-comer, as had been true with the other man, paced around and around the grave, trying to find a way out but couldn't. In the pitch dark, the pacing man hadn't seen the other man crouched in a corner. Finally, the sitting man got up and approached the new-comer from behind, tapping him on the shoulder and saying in a sepulchral voice, "You can't make it, buddy." Then Grandpa's voice leaped into the long-awaited punch line: *"BUT HE DID!"* And we'd roar, even us kids, by now playing over by the fireplace with the blocks. And stories and jokes would continue to be told—and we never tired of hearing them.

When there was a break in the action, Grandma would give us haircuts. In those early days there was no motor attached to the clippers as is true today but, rather, each time Grandma squeezed the handles together, a sheaf of hair would fall. But those of us who were down the line a bit had to endure the heat generated by the ever hotter clippers; worse yet, Grandma would occasion-ally yank hair out by its roots—and we would howl or scream, to no avail, because Grandma could not hear our wails—she could only read lips.

At night after supper, everyone would gather round the piano and sing. Grandma would gravitate over to the piano, put her hand on the soundboard, and seraphically smile as she *felt* the music! Later yet games would be brought out, and Grandpa would challenge all comers to caroms—and he'd whop most of his sons. If they didn't let us kids play games with them, we'd play with the blocks.

Eventually, to the sounds of slammed car doors, good-byes, shooing away cats, crunching gravel, and tears, the clan would drive away, one car at a time.

And so it went, season after season. Each time we came, before

I opened the gate, I'd turn and gaze longingly up the hill toward the lost Shangri-la beyond the three gates. In all the years that followed, I could only bear to return once, but it was not the same: A multimillionaire from San Francisco lived there now and had built something at the top of the hill that made me cry when I saw it.

Awareness came back to me gradually. The house was still silent, so my conscious mind picked up where it would rather not have. I remembered when it seemed—because of the battering of the years—best that Grandpa and Grandma should leave their Napa Valley garden spot and move north to Oregon so my only double relatives (my father's youngest brother, Warren, had married my mother's youngest sister, Jeannie) could be near enough to take care of them.

But now the rest of the family no longer came on holidays, and the Oregon coastal mist and rain kept Grandma inside a lot. I came to that house only twice, and each time I did so, it was not the same—not at all the same! They seemed a hundred years older than they had before. I did not see the blocks—I was too old to want to play with them anyhow. Gone was the vitality, the, what the Spanish call *chispa,* that made being with them such an adventure. Then Grandpa just let go—and not too long afterward, Grandma, bereft of her lifeline into the speaking world, followed him.

By now I had a wife and children of my own and was far too busy to dwell much in the past. But there came a time, some years later, when I began to remember. When I belatedly realized that, of all the things our family had ever possessed, I longed for only one thing: *those blocks!* I wondered if they had by now been thrown away: Who, after all, in this hectic life we live, would care much about an ancient basket of battered-looking blocks?

It took years, though—years of wondering about those blocks along the long corridors of the night—before I posed a question in a letter to my aunt and uncle, a question I wasn't sure I wanted to hear the answer to: "Those old blocks we used to play with— if they still exist, what do you say to giving a few to each grand-child who used to play with them?" The question was rhetorical: I didn't really expect an answer . . . and I didn't get one.

But in recent days, weeks, and months, I had found myself more and more often carried back to that time so many years before, to that time when those blocks were the most important thing in the world to me, the most prized, the most *loved*. Funny how it takes so many years in life before you realize value: If the house caught on fire, what you'd race for first.

I heard my aunt come in . . . and my heart began shuddering: *Did I really want to know?*

In the end, even if the blocks were gone forever, I just *had* to know!

So, struggling to keep my voice from shaking, I asked the fate-ful question: "Aunt Jeannie . . . , you remember . . . uh . . . uh . . . those . . . uh . . . ."

"Ye-e-s," she answered.

"Well, uh . . . uh . . . it's about the . . . the . . . uh . . . *blocks* we used to play with, so many years ago. Uh . . . uh . . . I was just curious . . . what ever happened to them?"

Matter-of-factly, my aunt ended the uncertainty of the years: "The old blocks? They're fine. They're here."

"They're *here,* in *this house?*" I sputtered inanely.

"Yes. They're here."

Pausing to regain my equilibrium, I finally managed to say, "Uh . . . do you mind if . . . *Can I see them?*"

"Of course. Come with me."

In her bedroom, in the back of her closet, was a strangely

familiar brown wicker basket. Filled with old blocks. She picked it up and took it into the living room, then handed it to me.

I was so stupefied I could not talk. Lord Carnarvon himself, on first stepping into King Tutankhamen's tomb in Egypt's Valley of the Kings, could not have been more overcome than I—I, who had long since given up the blocks as lost forever!

I just stared at them stupidly, unable to say anything that made sense. Finally, I sighed, *I'd give almost anything for these!*

My aunt smiled for the first time.

Time passed, and I continued to fondle them, unable to stop touching them. Finally, I asked her if she'd ever thought about my request years before.

Instantly, she said that she had, and that the answer was no.

Then, seeing my woebegone face, a smile as big as Texas spread across her dear face:

"But *you* can have them if you wish."

"If I *wish?*" I gasped out.

"Yes, but there are conditions."

"What?" I demanded.

"That they always stay together, that they are never divided, that they remain in the family *always* . . . and that—" and here her smile grew even broader—"only when you find someone who loves them as much as you do . . . can you let them go."

Returning home, I carried those precious blocks with me into the passenger cabin, not daring to risk checking them on the plane.

A few days ago, for the first time in my life, I really analyzed the basket of blocks I had for so long taken for granted. The basket itself is most likely well over a century old. In it there is an ivory-ish shoehorn, a very old darning sock egg, and an accumulation of seventy-three blocks, representing at least six generations: twenty-two uncolored alphabet blocks (one, perhaps the oldest, has burn holes in each of four sides) dating back to the early 1800s. These are so old that the corners have been worn round by generations of children playing with them; one single *A* block, with color, dating to around the 1850s; twelve multi-colored picture blocks (forming a design on each side) dating back to the 1870s; four very small blocks with raised figures dating back to around 1890; twenty-two alphabet blocks with raised colored lettering, dating back to about 1910; and one modern nondescript colored block dating back to the 1940s—how it got into the box I haven't the slightest idea. Apparently, each family for over a century added blocks to the basket. Undoubtedly, a number have been lost during the family's many peregrinations: from Massachusetts to New Hampshire to western New York to California (not long after the Civil War), then many moves criss-crossing California afterward.

In the end, I concluded that I was glad I didn't really know for sure how old they were. It was enough that my only surviving great-aunt, memory razor-sharp in her mid-nineties, remembers playing with the blocks and thinking them "very old" even then. Are they per chance two hundred years old? I don't know. Were they played with by a distant cousin, Buffalo Bill Cody? I don't know. And the tree the oldest blocks came from? Was it standing during the Revolutionary War? Was it standing when the Pilgrims landed in 1620? I don't know . . . but it could *have been*.

In researching block history, I discovered that alphabet blocks date clear back to the 1600s, John Locke first advocating their use in his landmark educational book, *Some Thoughts Concerning Education,* 1693. Thereafter, alphabet blocks were known as "Locke's Blocks." They crossed the Atlantic and were played with by American children during Colonial times; by the mid-1800s thousands of middle- and upper-class American families owned such block sets as those earliest blocks in our family basket.

Friedrich Froebel, one of the German founders of kindergarten education, urged the adoption of alphabet blocks in that curriculum, which really hit full stride in America late in the nineteenth century (Andrew McClary's *Toys with Nine Lives: A Social History of American Toys,* North Haven, Connecticut: The Shoe String Press, 1997).

But, more to the point, why do these simple little blocks mean so much to people like me? Perhaps the best answer is found in Dan Foley's wondrous book *Toys through the Ages* (Philadelphia: Chilton Brooks, 1962): "The magic land of childhood, which was filled with delight, vanished with the approach of adolescence, so, too, did the toys. Only a small fragment of the millions of toys made in times past, even during the last century, remain to bestir our nostalgia and to record the heritage of childhood." Foley then quotes Odell Shepard, who wrote in *The Joys of Forgetting* (Boston: Houghton Mifflin, 1929): "Our toys were almost idols. There was a glamour upon them which we do not find in the more splendid possessions of our late years, as though a special light fell on them through some window of our hearts that is now locked up forever. . . . We loved them with a devotion such as we shall never feel again for any of the things this various world contains, be they ever so splendid or costly."

―――――――――――――――――――

A few weeks ago our Grey House high in the Colorado Rockies was about as Christmassy as a house can get: On a ledge was Dickens's Christmas Village; on the mantel, twelve stockings; in a far corner, a tall evergreen, ablaze with ornaments and lights. Outside on the deck, our multicolored lights could be seen from ten miles away. But, for me, there was something that meant more than all these things together:

Yes, there was Taylor, our first grandchild; only seven months old, but intent on toppling the tree so that he could suck on each branch. Short of that, if he'd had his way, the lower three feet of decorations would have been stripped bare. The only thing he showed comparable interest in were the blocks. He drooled on them, he sucked on them, and he took fiendish delight in swatting down the block towers we made for him. I can hear his joyful chortle yet! I would guess him to be one of the first children to have played with those blocks during the last third of a century (quite likely, our son, Greg, was one of the last to have played with them during the late 1960s).

So it was that as I watched Taylor play, I felt a soothing sense of the continuity of life, of the past joining hands with the present, of a long procession of ancestors magically shedding their wrinkles and beards, gray hair and hoop skirts, and all plopping themselves down on the floor with the blocks, as children once again.

As for Taylor, I wondered if he'd love them as much as *I* did, as *they* did. Probably not, for our generations (even I was a Depression baby) had very few things to play with, compared to the king's ransom in toys we shower upon children today. Which makes me wonder: *Perhaps we were lucky, for we appreciated what little we had.*

So it is that never can I look at this basket of blocks without memories flooding in upon me—memories of Taylor; myself; my son, Greg; my father; my grandfather; and a host of faded tintype-photograph ancestors. Given that intergenerational bond, somehow it does not seem far-fetched at all to me, to imagine Grandma greeting her homecoming family in the New Earth by saying, "You *dear* soul!" to each of us, then turning to Grandpa with "Why, Papa"—and Grandpa turning to me and saying, "Joe . . . did you . . . uh . . . uh . . . by any chance, bring the blocks?"

THE CASTLE-BUILDER

A gentle boy, with soft and silken locks,
A dreamy boy, with brown and tender eyes,
A castle-builder, with his wooden blocks,
And towers that touch imaginary skies.

A fearless rider on his father's knee,
An eager listener unto stories told
At the Round Table of the nursery,
Of heroes and adventures manifold.

There will be other towers for thee to build;
There will be other steeds for thee to ride;
There will be other legends, and all filled
With greater marvels and more glorified.

Build on, and make thy castles high and fair,
Rising and reaching upward to the skies;
Listen to voices in the upper air,
Nor lose thy simple faith in mysteries.

Henry Wadsworth Longfellow

The woodcut illustration on page 207 was created to go with this Longfellow poem when first published in *Young Folks* (one of the earliest child annual books in American history), vol. 3, 1867.